T O

R R

L A

M O

CURBSIDE SPLENDOR / CHICAGO

O W

N D

T O

R R

R

L A

M O O W N D

TEN STORIES BY JOSEPH BATES

CURBSIDE SPLENDOR PUBLISHING

Published by Curbside Splendor Publishing, Inc., Chicago, Illinois in 2013.

First Edition
Copyright © 2013 by Joseph Bates
Library of Congress Control Number: 2013944592

ISBN 978-0-9888258-1-9
Edited by Traci Kim
Designed by Alban Fischer

Manufactured in the United States of America.

www.curbsidesplendor.com

FOR MY FAMILY

MIRRORVERSE

M

y editor walks over on a Friday afternoon carrying a contraption that looks like you'd torture a spy with it. He clunks the thing down on my desk one-handedly by its metal neck.

"Project for you," he says. "Need a quick review."

I write tech and gadget news for a dying print newspaper in a medium-sized city.

"What the hell is it?" I ask.

"This," he says, "is the Belton Multiverse Spectrometer," craning his head to read the stamp on the side. Of course that doesn't tell me much. It has oculars like a two-socket microscope, but the body resembles an ammo box, with curly wires coming off like you'd expect to find on a moonshine still, and a few round dials on the front of it, and a couple of rectangular controllers with thin cords connected to the sides. It's like a mess of different machines soldered together in a vague turkey shape.

"It looks like junk," I say.

"It's ugly, for sure," he says, shrugging. "Yeah, you'll probably have to mention that in your review. Maybe find a euphemism—*retro-style*, or something—though the company swears it'll be sleeker and newer-looking when 2.0 hits the market."

"Okay," I say. "But what the hell is a Multiverse Spectrometer?"

"It sees multiverses," my editor says, as if this should have been obvious. "You know. Like in the DC comic books."

That's all he had to say; I understood him then. It's the theory that there's not just one universe but many, all coexisting at once, and that in these other universes, events unfold in slightly or drastically different ways than in ours. In fact, if I understand the theory right, and take it to its logical conclusion, it means that everyone is everything and everyone else. We all go through every possible permutation of life throughout the Multiverse. There are universes, in other words, where I am a murderer, and others where I am the murdered, others where I'm a famous rock star or can move objects with my mind, and many others where I'm just sitting in a room somewhere wasting my life, like I'm doing right now.

"Just to be clear," I confirm, "you mean it looks into alternate universes?"

"Retails for $699, MSRP," he says. He wipes his machine-hand on his pants. "It sure is ugly, though. You're right about that."

"I didn't realize that the Multiverse theory had been proven."

"That's why you're the gadget guy," my editor says, "and not the science guy. The technology was invented by Belton back in the '50s, intended for military use—that's why it looks like it does, I guess, meant to help blow shit up, not look good on a coffee table—but the army couldn't use it. They wanted to show possible outcomes of a potential action or whatever, to see if their plan would work, so they'd look into the Multiverse and find a universe where they took the same action and then they'd watch how it played out. But it was useless, since instead of showing them one outcome, it showed every outcome. Some universes where the action succeeded and a bunch more where it was bullshit, and others where everyone in the room spontaneously combusted. It's pretty cool, but I can see how it'd be plain useless in that regard."

"Am I supposed to like this new product, or not?"

This is a standard question.

"Belton's letting us keep it," my editor says, "so like it about seven stars out of ten. I want it back when you're done. You've got to admit, it's an amazing concept. Should change the way we look at the world, right?"

"But what will people use it for?" I pick it up by the neck. It's heavy as a dumbbell.

"Oh, I don't know," he says honestly. "People'll probably use it to stream porn. But you watch it like TV. Look through the little eyeholes there, or you can hook it up to a monitor or TV set. It's got RCA and HDMI outputs in the back, and it's Bluetooth ready, which is a nice touch. I had it running through my Xbox for a while last night and tried to play multiplayer across the Multiverse, which would've been awesome. Play against myself from some other universe and rocket-propel-grenade myself to hell. But I couldn't get it to work. It's not much of a gaming system. Anyway, I need eight hundred words by Monday, and about seven and a half stars. I don't know if I mentioned it, but they're paying us for a decent review. So there's that."

"So it's an advertisement," I say.

"It's a reviewvertisement," he says.

"What if I have plans this weekend? You didn't even bother to ask. It's kind of late on a Friday to be bringing me something like this, isn't it?"

"Ahh," he says, crossing his arms and smiling. "So it's Secret Girlfriend Weekend, huh?"

Secret girlfriend is what he calls my ex-wife Marlene. Every couple of weeks, Marlene comes over and watches an old movie with me on a Friday night. Her husband travels a lot, so it's just her and their two kids most of the time. Her old girlfriends have all moved off to other places, so it's me she turns to. She hires a sitter and comes over, and we watch black-and-white movies we never got to watch when we were married, because of all the drama. Good company, that's all it is. But as soon as my editor learned about it, he started calling her my secret girlfriend, as if we were up to something that her husband doesn't know about. Which is completely untrue: nothing is up between us, so there's really no need for her husband to know anything.

We've rekindled a friendship in the past year or so. Coffee every couple of months, that was all at first. Then, for the last three months, we've been watching movies at my place without telling her traveling husband exactly where she is.

Good company, that's all.

"That's none of your business," I tell him, a little too quickly.

"Touchy, touchy," he says. "You're carrying the torch, buddy. It's kind of sad to see. Plenty of women out there. Anyway, don't look so glum. There's probably some universe where you're the boss and I'm the lowly writer, and you've just come over and given me a crap assignment for the weekend. So it's karma. It all comes out in the wash. What an elegant universe. As for your plans, just incorporate the machine into your date night. You can use it just like cable TV, only better. Hey, put that in the review! Find a universe of erotic pleasures or something, and you two can watch it together on your couch and pretend not to be turned on by it. Then she'll leave, and you'll be frustrated and confused, and it'll be just like your usual Friday night."

THE PIZZA GUY shows up while I'm still trying to hook the Multiverse Spectrometer to my TV. I pay him and put the pizza out on the kitchen table next to the bottle of wine. Then I go back to the living room to fiddle with the device some more. I'm getting nothing but gray-white fuzz, but according to the manual, that's what I'm supposed to get. The manual explains that the fuzz between channels on a television is actually radiation left over from the Big Bang in a state of cooling, which I never knew, and it's inside this cosmic fuzz that I'm going to view other universes. But even reading the manual, it's not immediately clear how you're supposed to operate the thing: There's the Nintendo-looking controller, which I guess you can use to scroll universes or save the princess from the tower. The oversized dull chrome dials on front, which fine-tune the picture of the universes, and a small keypad no bigger than a cigarette pack attached by a cord the thickness of a whip of licorice.

I pick up the keypad and press the home button, just to see what happens.

A search box comes up, cursor blinking. It may be my imagination, but it seems like as soon as the box appears, the air in my living room gets ionized, charged up. The lint on my sweater stands up straight. I've got the box stretched from the television to my coffee table, the curled wires a dangerous obstruction, the whole thing uglying the place. I hear a faint hum and wonder how much radiation this thing puts out. I also wonder what's going to happen when I enter a search term and open space-time in my living room. The wiring in my apartment isn't ideal.

I could wait for Marlene to find out, but that blinking cursor has me intrigued. Everything in the Multiverse has already happened, if the machine does what it says—that means there's a universe where all wars were won by the opposite side as in ours, or where Oswald saves JFK's life using the Heimlich, or Abraham Lincoln becomes a high-seas pirate, or Napoleon could not be defeated because his skin was made of diamonds. I'm holding the little keypad—my thumb feels very fat across the letters, I note for the review—and I begin typing in not "Lincoln Pirate" or "Napoleon Diamond Skin" but my own name and a plus sign, and Marlene's married name. I put in today's date.

I've begun to realize that it's only a matter of time before my ex-wife and I end up in bed together. It's true that our coffees were purely platonic, and further true that nothing has happened between us since we've foregone the coffees to watch old movies in my apartment on Friday nights. We eat pizza. We drink wine. We enjoy Bogey and Bacall. We sit on the couch so close that it's like our legs are touching, though they're not, and there's always a bunch of couch on either side of us that goes unused. We sit so close I can feel the energy of her thigh on mine. We have a certain electricity between us, as real as the radiation coming off this metal box, and maybe as dangerous. If we make popcorn instead of order pizza, our hands brush each other's as we reach for a handful.

And there's also the fact that she's been telling me things here lately . . . mostly how she's been unhappy with Brian since the arrival of their second child. How he's never at home, and it's like she's raising the kids all by herself. She's been opening up, I guess you'd say, telling me how she feels about her life and marriage, and I've been there for her.

I think we both know where this is headed.

We're maybe three old movies away from crawling into bed and making a big mistake. One of those much-needed, both-feeling-vulnerable, pay-for-it-later-but-enjoy-it-right-now big mistakes.

It could be tonight.

I glance up at the clock—she'll probably be ringing the bell in five or six minutes. Hardly enough time to do a search for us, to see what might happen when she comes over, but I've got us typed into the machine already and think I can do this quickly. Just take a peek. It doesn't occur to me that there might be no way to clear the search history until I've already hit ENTER, but by then it's too late.

I hit ENTER.

An icon flashes on the screen and spins, sending the air into more invisible crackles. Then, I'm not sure how else to say this, I feel myself breach the unseen membrane of the universe. Nothing visible or obvious, no streaming special effects like in *2001*, but it feels like the floor is sliding away from me, and my feet are pincushioning, and I think I'm going to be sick. Then the fuzz on the screen changes into ghosts, and the ghosts become forms, my equilibrium rights itself, and there I am on my television set, sitting on my couch with the Nintendo controller in my hand, staring back at myself dumbly. Wearing the same clothes I am now (sweater and slacks, which I wore to work). It looks like a mirror image of me, same expression and everything, and for a moment I think that I've dialed up the very universe I'm in. I knit my brow, and so does he; I wave, and so does he. We're a Marx Brothers routine.

But then the apartment buzzer rings in the universe on the television, and this mirror image forgets all about me. He puts the controller down, rubs his sweaty hands on his slacks, adjusts his belt, and goes to answer the door. Nothing but couch on the screen for a few seconds, though I keep watching, and then two pairs of legs come into view, facing each other. Very close, not only in an embrace but, I can tell from the wobble of the legs, in the midst of a passionate, face-sucking kiss. Their hands start sliding all over each other, down thighs, reaching around to cup each other's behinds.

I am watching myself and my ex-wife make out in another universe.

They lower onto the couch, with me stretched out on my back and Marlene climbing on top, really going at it. And while this should make me feel funny, watching them like this, perhaps even envious at how boldly they're making their mistake, I am instead filled with a kind of wonderful anticipation and fear that makes my stomach float.

There's nothing to say I'm not looking at the path my own night could take.

Right on cue, my own apartment's buzzer goes off. Marlene.

I scramble for the controller, my first impulse being to hide what I'm watching . . . but then it occurs to me I could just let it play. I could always act embarrassed when Marlene comes in, if she's offended by it, but then what if she's not? What if she looks at us making out in another universe, then looks over at me and says, This is what I've been hoping for.

Yes, I know.

I've mistaken this marvelous machine for Cinemax.

Meanwhile, on my television, Marlene and I are fumbling with our buttons. No talking, no overthinking. I can hear their breaths getting more rapid. It's almost embarrassing. Maybe it'll be good for a laugh between us, me and my Marlene, if it doesn't lead to anything else.

So I risk it and leave it running. I go hit the buzzer to let her past the security door, then I do one last check of my hair, teeth, and breath.

I look at myself in the bathroom mirror and say, What are you doing, dummy? Then I go let her in, to find out.

Only it is not Marlene at my front door.

It's Brian. Marlene's husband.

He's standing there in a raincoat with light snowflakes on the shoulders, and he has what might be described as an unpleasant, murderous look on his face.

"Mind if I come in?" he tells me.

I step back and he comes inside, brushes a bit of snow onto my floor. Then he kind of walks through the foyer and into my dining room, peers into the kitchen. I see him take note of the table, the pizza box, the wine, and the two wineglasses. He turns back to look at me.

"What's going on between you and Marlene?" he asks.

I have a couple of ways to play this: I can act dumb and say, What do you mean? Or, I can answer honestly and say, Brian, I have no idea.

"What do you mean?" I say.

"She came clean with me about you and her," he says. "She told me everything."

Of course there's not much to tell. We haven't crossed a line, at least not physically. Emotionally, perhaps, and I wonder if Marlene has told him that these Friday nights are important to her in some way. That she needs them. That would be nice to hear. But I don't know what she's told him. Whatever it is, it's lead Brian to drive all the way across town to kill me. Maybe he doesn't know anything and he's just fishing for information. He thinks he's got his hook in me.

Still, it doesn't take a genius to know that this has the potential to get out of hand.

"Look, I don't know what Marlene has told you . . . "

"She told me she's been over here when I'm out of town." He's looking around the place, fists on his sides like a father in a '50s TV show. "She said you two've been snuggling up on the couch, sitting close, getting cozy. She said you have a certain electricity—"

"Really? She said that?"

"—and that's all she'll own up to," he says. "But I know that's not all. She's at home right now, crying her eyes out. That's a sign. You can't tell me it's not. People don't cry for no reason."

I want to tell him that's not true. Especially not for Marlene. He ought to know that by now.

"Shouldn't you be out of town?" I ask, not meaning for this to come out as high-pitched as it does.

He turns his whole torso around, elbows in Vs, surveying the dining room. There's that paternal air about him that makes me feel guilty as hell. He looks at the floors, in the corners of the room, at my bookshelf, and finally back to me.

"Am I going to find condoms here?" he asks.

I say, "Are you going to *look*?"

I've always kind of liked Brian, the few times I've met him. He seems like a generally kindhearted man, like he loves Marlene. I'd actually done a pretty good job of not thinking much about him, and I'd certainly never asked her what she tells him when she comes over. To bring it up would've been to bring it out in the open, then to have a serious talk, with the end result that our Friday nights together would go away. I sure didn't want that.

"Look, Brian," I say, "I realize this looks funny, but there's nothing going on. I can promise you that. Nothing but good company, that's all.

With you out of town all the time, Marlene just needs to get out of the house . . . I don't know why she's so upset, really, or what she's crying about. We haven't done anything for her to be ashamed of."

Thank God this is true, not so much as an open-mouthed kiss between us. And thank God I didn't add *yet* to the end of that, like I almost did.

"She's done something enough to cry about," he says to me. "She was so bad off I cancelled my flight to Boston. She's sorry for something, but when I press her for specifics, she won't say anything."

"Because there are none to tell," I say. "So maybe she should've told you where she was, sure, and honestly, I don't know why she didn't"—and I feel immediately bad for implicating Marlene a little here—"but I promise you, on my word, that there is nothing untoward, nothing more than just good friendship, going on between me and her. I can promise you that."

Then, Brian and I hear Marlene moan loudly from the direction of my living room.

His eyebrows clench down into little eyebrow fists.

"What was that?" he says.

"What was what?"

"Ohhhhh yesssssss," Marlene calls out.

"Oh," I say. "Do you mean that?"

Before I can think of an excuse for what that could possibly be— alarm clock?—Brian's stomping back toward the living room, and I'm following behind slowly. By the time I'm in there with him, he's standing in front of the set, back to me, and doesn't appear to be moving at all.

Just standing there, fists on his hips, shoulders up and tense, watching.

This is the moment, I realize, where this particular universe is about to take a turn. Where Brian pulls a gun out of his overcoat and shoots me dead, or turns around and lunges toward me and chokes me. Where we end up on the eleven o'clock news, and they'll probably interview my editor at the paper, and he'll look into the camera with that told-you-so smile I hate, and he'll say, "Dude had a secret girlfriend, and it was his ex-frikkin-wife. How'd he *think* this was gonna turn out?"

"So I can explain this," I say weakly, though I'm not sure that's true. "There's this theory, see—well, I guess it's not a theory anymore—there's this thing where . . . see, there are these parallel universes . . . "

But Brian doesn't appear to be listening. Nor, to my surprise, does he whip around to get his hands on my neck. Instead he puts his arms down and lets his shoulders drop, then he turns to face me, his whole body suddenly slack and deflated, as if the pressure of having to puff himself up for a fight, grind his jaw at me, has exhausted him.

His voice is very timid when he speaks.

"You had your chance," he says, measuring his words. No rage in his voice, but loss and hurt. "You had Marlene for *five* years," he says, "and had your life with her, and you blew it. Now she's got a family, children . . . and I'm not always there for her, I realize that . . . "

"You're gone way too much," I agree, hoping to put some of this back on him, as a way of saving my cowardly hide.

But Brian actually nods when I say it.

"I know that," he says. "I haven't been the best husband, I know."

"You really haven't," I say.

"But make no mistake I love her . . . " and then his voice trails off, like he's going to get emotional. I see it threatening to cloud his face, and I feel embarrassed for him. For us both. Then he says, composing himself, "And I'm not going to lose her. Not to anyone, and certainly, certainly not to *you*. I'm going to do better. I guess it took something like this to finally . . . but, back to you. You had your chance with her already. That's over and done with. She told me how you were in the marriage, by the way. You weren't exactly Mr. Attentive. I'm not going to have you coming around now, confusing her. Taking advantage of our problems. From this moment on, I don't want you anywhere near her or my family. Got it?"

There's really not much I can do, except for agree. And of course I've known this moment was coming. I just didn't figure on it so soon, and especially not like this. An affair that ended before it ever began.

"Okay," I say. My throat is so dry, the word comes out in a little scratch. "I understand."

"Good," he says, then he pauses a moment and adds, which seems strange to me, "Thank you."

And just like that, Brian and I have run out of things to talk about. He tightens his coat and pulls his collar up, then walks back through my apartment and lets himself out. It feels weird to have someone leave without a goodbye, to simply stop talking and exit, but that's what he does. And it's what I've done, too. Not so much as a goodbye to my ex-wife, after all we've been through. But I suppose one could argue that we've had our fair share of goodbyes already. Maybe more than our fair share.

THOUGH THERE IS ANOTHER UNIVERSE, just a dial-switch away, where Marlene and I maintain a lifelong love affair behind her callous husband's back, with an intensity never achieved by married couples. That forbidden angle, like in *The Thorn Birds*. Another flip of the dial finds us in a trailer park in Alabama, Marlene in perpetual curlers and me on the perpetual couch, and in another, we are in feudal Japan, samurai, and have been hired by third parties to bring them the severed head of one another. These third parties, it seems, could both be Brian.

In others, Marlene and I simply lose touch along the way, too distracted by the people and problems in our lives to think much about what we once had.

Then there are a multitude of universes—like the stars—where my ex-wife and I hold a completely average and insecure love affair, careless in what we're doing, sometimes hurtful to each other by accident, or on purpose. Where we don't always seem to be having a whole lot of fun. These bear a resemblance to the universe we live in now, though I keep this observation to myself.

But it's the universe of the almost-affair that really gets to her. Especially Brian's monologue in my living room, where he professes his love for her while standing in front of what he believes to be our recorded lovemaking, and where I back down, agree to get out of the way. As soon as he begins his speech, Marlene starts to sniff, dab her eyes with a Kleenex. We watch the whole thing about three times, at her request.

"I'm sorry," she says, fixing her mascara with her fingertip. Then she laughs. "I must be vulnerable tonight. It's just so beautiful. It bowls me over to hear that coming out of Brian's mouth."

"Hey," I say. "You want to go home? Are you feeling bad?"

"Oh, no," she says, wiping her nose with the tissue. "That Brian's not my Brian. Not by a long shot. But it's still lovely."

"Did you see us on that television?" I say, hoping to lighten the mood. "We looked pretty good naked together, huh?"

"Keep dreaming, buddy," she sniffles, and laughs again. "That's never going to happen."

But then she nudges her leg a bit closer to mine.

"Well, look," I say, "we can always go back to the goofy stuff, if you like."

By which I mean the universes we were watching before we started searching for ourselves—a universe where Alexander the Great has heat vision, or Neil Armstrong steps out of Apollo and gets beaten senseless by tiny moon people, or where Jesus and Moses fistfight. Like a giant Mad Lib made by God. Everything is possible and everything has happened, and it's only a matter of thinking of it and tuning it in. What an elegant universe.

But Marlene says no, she wants to keep watching the two of us on this contraption. And though neither of us says it, I think I understand why: it's because we don't know what we're doing here on these Friday nights when Brian's out of town. Or, we know certain things—that we enjoy one another's company, for example—but neither of us can say for sure why we're here. Maybe one of these flips of the dial will help us figure that out, will show us a version of ourselves that scares us into calling the whole thing off (and the one where Brian shows up at my apartment, I admit, has me thinking a little more soberly). Or we'll find one where the right thing to do is clear, and we do it, and everything about the way those lives play out seems so true and right, it allows us to know ourselves a little better, and to see ourselves out here, in this universe, more clearly. To know for certain what we do, and do not, want to happen, as if that universe and its stories had been written just for us.

GAS HEAD TELLS ALL

Q : Tell me, Gas Head, do you cry?

A: If you mean do I produce saline tears, then no. I weep a concentrated solution of gasoline and mucus that's actually closer to Napalm, so I've learned to keep it all in … I don't want to accidentally bomb a village. I'll never go on *Oprah*, let's say that much. [*Pause.*] That's a strange first question

Q: How old were you when you learned to keep your emotions in check?

A: From the beginning. As soon as I understood language. I think I knew *No-no-no-please-god* before *ma-ma*. My parents had a tough time of it when I was a baby. The concrete garage behind our house was converted into a nursery, and they added sprinklers and hoses and all that, and they still had the fire department out all the time. They knew all the firemen's names. Luckily, all I made were these little baby tears, or I might've torched the whole neighborhood.

Q: Hm.

A: So I learned to control myself early on. Sadness, anger, shame . . . I flare up when I get upset. Full-on rage, forget it. I blaze. I was on serotonin reuptake inhibitors before I reached preschool. I have to keep it tamped down, or there'll be trouble. Obviously talk radio is out for me. Election years, I don't even turn on the TV.

Q: And the last time you cried?

A: [*Long pause.*]

Q: Are you afraid to say?

A: There are people out there who want to blame me for things that aren't my fault. House fires, brush fires. I must have one of those guilty-looking faces. [*Laughs, flares up.*] I won't lie and say it's never happened, that I've never once cried in my thirty-some years. That wouldn't be human. But it's infrequent, I can assure you, and always safely contained.

Q: So you think of yourself as human?

A: What in the hell kind of question is that?

Q: Well, I—

A: Do you have any idea how offensive that is? Wow.

Q: I'm sorry, I didn't mean—

A: Have you ever asked anyone *else* in an interview if they were human?

Q: Gary Busey.

A: No. Not funny.

Q: I'm sorry. I didn't mean offense. But at the same time—

A: [*Dimming.*] No, no. It's okay. I guess I understand why you'd ask. It's just . . . you should be aware of how a question like that would sound to someone like me.

Q: Someone like you?

A: Okay, so there's no one like me. How it sounds to me.

Q: Let's shift gears. You've said that . . .

A: No, wait. I want to answer the question. First, let me ask you, what's it mean to be human?

Q: [*Pause.*] I'm not sure I'm qualified to say.

A: I was born. I suffer. I'm self-aware. I have the illusion of free will. One day I'll die.

Q: Yes, but does—

A: I pay the cable bill. My back hurts. I wish I drove a better car.

Q: But you've made some good money over the years, haven't you? You had a number of endorsements.

A: Sure. Kingsford, that was the big one. The Match-Lite charcoal people.

Q: And wasn't that profitable?

A: That money's gone. I burned right through it.

Q:

A: Back in the '80s, when Michael Jackson caught his head on fire shooting that Pepsi commercial, remember that? I did the Coke version and moonwalked around screaming. Well, not moonwalked, but I walked backwards and screamed and grabbed myself. That was the first, I think, the first commercial endorsement. It won some awards, but it was kind of mean-spirited, now that I look back.

Q: Coke is a big deal.

A: But see, all that money went to my parents. I was still a kid back then.

Q: And they mishandled the funds?

A: Enough has been written about that. I don't want to dredge that back up.

Q: Are you still in touch with them?

A: I understand it was hard having me. I wasn't what they expected or wanted. You want your son to grow up to be a pilot, not a pilot light. That's my little joke. They're just, they were simple folks, and they didn't expect what they got when they had me, but then they saw an opportunity to make something of their lives and get out of that town, and they did it. But I don't blame them for anything. I have no ill feelings.

Q: So you're not in touch with them?

A: Through my lawyer.

Q: They live out west now, is that right?

A: Yes.

Q: In L.A.?

A: Yes, I think that's right.

Q: So you had nothing to do with the Gas Head animated series a few years back?

A: Nothing at all. See, they were using my likeness without my permission.

Q: Your parents were.

A: Right, and . . .

Q: The presiding judge ruled your trademark-infringement lawsuit without merit.

A: Well, see, they called the main character Barry instead of Gas Head, and they changed some of the details around, such as the fact that Barry is happy and gets along with his parents. And the judge didn't really hear us out. He had it in for me from the beginning. Plus, my lawyer is a colossal piece of shit.

Q: Your parents countersued for defamation and emotional distress, and they won that.

A: [*Long pause.*] They did.

Q: In 2003, you were arrested for producing methamphetamines.

A: Trumped-up charge. They didn't have a case.

Q: So it was some kind of misunderstanding?

A: My house blew up, and I live in Muncie, Indiana, and if you live in Muncie and your house blows up, then you're probably cooking methamphetamine.

Q: And your house blew up because . . . ?

A: Because my head is a giant ball of gas that's on fire.

Q: Here's something I don't understand: how do you have eyes and teeth? Why don't they burn?

A: That's a dumb question. Obviously I don't have a clue why my eyeballs don't burn. They should pop like a campfire log. It's like asking me why my head is on fire. I'd love to know that myself. If I could figure out who to ask, or better yet who's responsible, believe me, there'd be words.

Q: Do you mean God?

A:

Q: Can you go swimming?

A: Oh, sure.

Q: Do you date?

A: Here and there. I do well in chat rooms. Sometimes I get a first date out of that. The second date, that's the question mark.

Q: Have you ever been in love?

A: Yes.

Q: Was the feeling returned?

A: Oh yes.

Q: And it was serious?

A: It was the most important time in my life.

Q: So what happened?

A: You mean, why did it end?

Q: Yes.

A: Why we broke up?

Q: Yes.

A: [*Pause.*] I guess we just grew apart.

Q: Is there anything else you'd like our readers to know?

A: I just finished my first album, available on my website, TheRealGashead.com. I take PayPal and personal check. If you only have cash, we can probably still work something out.

Q: Okay . . .

A: I recorded it on my own label, GH Records, so I could maintain artistic control. It's like the essence of me on the album, for people who want to know who the real Gas Head is. It's got some rockers on it, plus a few ballads. I co-wrote one of the songs with Mark McGrath from Sugar Ray.

Q: Anything else?

A: I'm still looking for that special lady I can spend my life with. Maybe if someone reads this and wants to be in touch, we could go out to dinner. Or you could come to my house, if that would be better for you. We could listen to the album.

Q: Alright . . .

A: If you sent me an email last week trying to order the album, the server went down and I lost everything. You'll have to log on again. I'm sorry. Oh, and there are t-shirts for sale on my website. Please buy from me, not from those other places on the web. 'Cause I won't see a dime from them. Thank you.

Q: Anything else?

A: I don't even know why we *have* these emotions, what good they are, if all they do is . . . they hurt you, and they hurt others, and then you just spend your whole life . . . It's like you have to find a way to numb them, to fight them down, just to get by.

Q: Anything else?

A: It's hard to put into words. I don't always understand what I feel. I guess I'm just looking for a connection, you know? A feeling like I'm not so alone.

Q: Anything else?

A: Like right now, for instance, I'm not even sure you're listening to me.

Q: Anything else?

A: I'll tell you this—there are times when I really want to cry. Just throw my head back and let go, even if I bring the whole goddamn world down with me.

HOW WE MADE A DIFFERENCE

On Halloween the neighborhood children dress up like neo-conservatives and go door-to-door spreading lies. This happens one Halloween out of every four. In other years they are cowboys with broomstick horses and toy guns drawn in stick-em-up-partner fashion, or ballerinas in tutus and tin-foil tiaras, bundled in red bulky overcoats they'd fought their moms not to wear. These years they're fine kids and can be reasoned with, and they deserve some name-brand candy. But every fourth, when the national elections heat up, their parents get hold of them and they become demoniacs for free enterprise and the white race. Their beady, innocent eyes steel-blue like the life has been syringed from them and replaced with the warm liquid metal of little fascist visions. See them coming toward you in unstoppable lines, from across streets, dressed in dark blue business suits (stupid for street safety) and drab businesswoman pantsuits with shoulderpads like right tackles. It's *Village of the Damned* dressed by the sales rack at Sears.

"You can't trust Bob Janney," these kids say. "He's a tax and spend liberal. Can I have a Snickers?"

"Did you know that Embryonic Stem Cell Research takes developing embryos from the still-growing wombs of unwed teen black mothers impregnated by Phil . . . by Phil Clinton?"

"It's *Bill*," their mothers whisper helpfully from my hedges. "*Bill* Clinton."

"Stay out of my hedges," I yell at them, "and keep your government hands off my body!" I add, even though I am a man.

Then, a Sugar Daddy for little Lisa, a bite-sized Twix for Jimmy, and one more fist pump for the Freedom Lover ruining my lawnscape. She flicks me back the one-fingered victory salute.

This is what passes for Halloween in my neighborhood.

I suppose I could love it or leave it, but I hate it and stay.

Where would I go? If I packed up the car and kept driving for a preponderance of the correct yard signs, I'd be in the Pacific Northwest somewhere. Like Vancouver. Who knows if they even celebrate Halloween way up there?

Back in the eco-friendly heat of my house, I have some *All Things Considered* on tape. I think about yanking the cassette that's running— screeching cat noises and ghost boos piped to my front porch—and cranking up some pensive news and commentary instead.

I think about razor-blading some apples, or perhaps my wrists.

Honey tells me if it bothers me so much, I shouldn't answer the door.

"That's not the point," I tell her. She's sitting at the kitchen table snipping coupons. I go stand in the kitchen doorway so I can talk to her and readjust the seam on my pelvic bone . . . I'm dressed in my spooky skeleton suit, a black leotard with the bones drawn on with puff paint. I've worn it the last five years running, and Honey thinks the worn-out bulges are becoming obscene. "Turning a blind eye won't stop this indoctrination," I say. "These are just children. They're supposed to *love* Halloween."

"I always did," she says.

She's moving the scissors horizontal, vertical, up, down, snip. Bargains relax her.

"Right, me too," I say. "I *loved* it."

Honey and I live an honest good life and do things right per the progressive worldview—we go eco-lightbulbs, we take out magazine subscriptions from every disadvantaged or handicapped kid who comes around, and I send a bunch of email forwards every day to raise awareness. But that also means we've chosen to go childless. How can we bring a child into the world, we think, with all this war and Orwellian whatnot? Back when I was a kid, Halloween was about candy, and Christmas was about presents, and politics was more like fencing or smoking cigars, civilized. Things made sense. Then politics became a no-limit, anything-goes steel-cage match, Christmas became culture wars and fake plastic baby Jesus, and Halloween became the stump. "'These knucklehead parents," I say again, "they're *ruining* it. We can't just bury our heads in the sand on this, Honey. We have to take wing! One day these kids will have kids of their own, and the cycle of indoctrination will continue. And that'll happen sooner rather than later, what with abstinence-only education."

"It's a mess," she says.

"Damn right," I say.

The doorbell moans like a ghoul.

"You're really setting yourself up for disappointment," Honey tries to tell me. "Maybe you should just boycott Halloween on election years."

That's one thing that disappoints me about Honey: her defeatist attitude.

"We've got to fight this enemy where we find them, baby," I tell her. "That's on our *own front porch!*"

I fiddle my pelvis back in place and practice my goofy skeleton two-step. I grab our big bowl of candy.

"Besides," I add, "maybe this one'll be more reasonable."

Honey mm-hmms in a way that illustrates doubt.

I leave the kitchen and dance my dem bones through the living room, dance up to the front door, open it wide, then I use my bone-chillingest skeleton voice: "Oooo-ooooooo, Haaaaaappy Halloweeeeeeeeen!"

Standing on my front porch is a pudgy pigsnout of a boy wrapped in bedhseets, carrying a plastic AK-47. He's painted himself in brownface, and there's a faded beach towel around his head in a turban.

I drop the skeleton act and stare.

"Now just what in the hell are you supposed to be?"

"I'm glad you asked me that, Mister," the boy says, revving up for his pitch. The dark foundation under his mouth has rubbed off in streaks where he's been chomping candy bars along the trail. "I'm Anytown Main Street USA, if Ted Booby gets elected."

He pauses for a response and takes my stunned disgust as an invitation to keep going.

"Did you know that right now there are Talibans in Toyota flatbed trucks waiting just outside the county line for the moment Ted Booby gets elected? As soon as that happens, why, there'll be Talibans all over this place, converting us to Islams and taking our factory jobs. Ted Booby's their *man*."

"Ted Booby's running for coroner," I tell the kid.

He thinks this over a second and picks nougat from his teeth. He scrunches his fat face like he's figuring math.

"Drumming up business," he says finally.

I take two rolls of Smarties and nail him right in the middle of the turban. "Get the hell out of here," I say. "You should be ashamed of yourself. Spreading hate like that."

The kid narrows his eyes at me and palms the barrel of his fake gun. If that conceal-carry passes, he'll be back. Instead he swallows his pride and reaches down for the candy, scoops it up, and then turns his fat ass back down toward the street.

Halfway down my drive, he turns around and yells, "You need Jesus, mister!"

"Booby for Coroner!" I yell back.

T HESE KIDS is all I can think while I watch the little Bubba in brownface shuffling back into foot traffic, as I watch the minivans and the wide urban assault vehicles pull up streetside and unload their propagandized little spawn. I'm indignant watching this, and all I can think is the same indignant mantra, *These kids*. I'm so indignant that I save it up until I'm back in the house, then I walk into the kitchen and let it fly:

"These kids!" I say.

"I know," Honey says.

"I mean, come on!"

"I *know* it."

Now she's doing crosswords. After that, she's got some reading lined up. She's put on her black cat ears I bought her, but she's drawn the line at the tail, barely participating.

It's not that she's apolitical; Honey's got the funk. She's had it for years, ever since that one election, the one we don't talk about, what with the protests and disputes, the courts getting involved, the families not speaking to each other, the late-night comics unsure whether to make fun of it all or run for the hills . . . then the riots, the marches dispersed by tear gas, and finally the National Guard called out to restore order. Ever since then it's been a very different world. Everything's politics. Red or blue, choose your side, nothing in between.

I might not complain, I realize, if the politics were a little saner and to my liking.

Back in our first-together days, Honey and I used to have so much fun, so much in common, such passion—we would canvas bad neighborhoods for our good candidates, then spend nights close in bed with our bodies curled up into a question mark. Sunday morning talk shows led to cuddling and footsie. Now when we hug each other, it's like we're ready for a bomb to go off. I've seen Honey face down lunks twice her size (twice mine) while out rocking the vote, watched her stand up to Right-to-Work anti-union thugs who were harassing our town's hardworking, salt-of-the-earth pro-union thugs, but since that election she's been a different person. But people deal with trauma in different ways, I guess; I get so mad I could shit myself, whereas Honey just folds inward and withdraws. She's got a back drawer full of campaign buttons from failed tickets that she keeps hidden away shameful like porn. She finally peeled the bumper stickers of yesterday's promises off the trunk of her car because she was tired of being pulled over for going two miles below the speed limit. One still barely reads "America Can Do Better," but only if you squint.

"Why don't you just put the candy out in a bucket and let the kids take it?" she asks. "You're not going to change anyone's mind by hitting someone's child with a sucker. Look, if you really need to do something, why not put out some literature? How about that Howard Zinn book? You've got, like, how many copies of that one? Four? Five? Maybe they'll take it, and their parents will read it, and you can actually make a difference. I'm afraid you're going to get arrested."

"You really think these people can be reasoned with?" I ask.

It's not a dare, but it sure sounds like one.

The doorbell groans in agony.

"Okay," she says, getting up from the kitchen table, taking the bowl of candy from me. "I'll give it a try. After this, it's bucket time."

She walks out of the kitchen and the door swings back my direction, like a saloon door before a gunfight. I steady it and put my ear bones against it. I hear Honey open the front door, then muffling sounds. No trick or treat. I hear a little voice sounding out the syllables in *activist judges*. Honey says something about the 7th U.S. Circuit Court of Appeals, and I hear a fake ray gun going off in a D-battery blaze. Then silence. One second later, I jump back from the kitchen door in time for her to kick it open.

"Those little fucking fascists!" she screams out. "Did you hear what that foul-mouthed little fuck called me?"

"What is it?" I ask, amazed at seeing her in such a state.

"There's no *hope*," she says. She's almost sputtering. "There's just no talking."

"What did he say?"

"You're right, you're right, you can't change those minds," she says. "There's no mind to change, nothing you can do with that stupidity . . . why are the only people having kids these dumb fuckers? Their kids are just like 'em. It's part of their plan. It's like we're being *bred out!*"

I haven't seen her this worked up in a long, long time. Her cat ears are hanging over to one side like she's baffled by some dangling string, and that shallow breath of hers is heaving, rhythmic, filling the whole room and tickling my lungs, sliding right down my thighs like loving fingers. Her face is flush and her neck, her entire body, is in that frenzied state of fight of flight, blushing with furious red splotches—"I mean, *come on!*"—and this sight of her standing there, squirming in her clothes, stirs in me something that'd been sleeping for too long and suddenly knows it's awake and alive.

And then it happens.

I have a vision, right there in my kitchen. It could be the adrenaline pumping candy-sugar into my heartbeat but I am having a vision like an ecstatic.

I see Honey—some future version of her—and she's plump with our own baby, holding a hand atop the curve of her stomach calm as a Madonna, rubbing softly and whispering words like *inclusion* and *middle class* and *progressivism*, and her boobs are huge, and I see myself down there on my knees, belly-level, with my head up against her, listening with all the care and attention of a safecracker. Then I see the vision fast forward: first steps and first birthdays and such, then that first Halloween. Dressed like a little baby shit-raker, like a little baby savior, dressed in a little baby onesie that says The System Is Whack and tiny sunglasses too cool for school. We'd be door to door, knocking and getting candy, changing lives.

"What's that look?" Honey says. She's still heaving but beginning to slow down, staring at me confused.

But I'm still seeing things. I'm looking over a bridge into the future at the strange shapes waving to me from the other side: Elementary school elections with platforms for more ice cream and longer recess and ending world hunger. Middle school debate team, earning the A plus plus phenom grade reserved for freakish prodigies. High school hallways passing out fliers that she—a she!—made with PhotoCrop, while other girls her age are still cutting out hairless heartthrobs from *Teen Beat*. On the fliers she's put war-torn grisly pictures in a collage of severed body parts and a slogan for peace that gets me called in for conference with the Principal.

"What *is* it?"

But I can't stop. The vision keeps on coming.

Local Town Council Baby, where she tears those Christian uptights and bun-hairs a new asshole.

State Senate Baby and U.S. Congress Baby, where her legislation is feared and reformist and kind.

National Election Baby—tell me why not?—and the cameras at her convention speech find Honey and me in the balcony, looking old and distracted by the lights but still proud. We take each other's papery hands and hold tight.

"What's that look?" Honey asks again. Then she gets a look on her face like she knows. "Oh, wait just a minute here," she says. "Maybe we should think this through."

But it's too late: the skeleton suit's on the floor, the bowl of candy on the floor, and a second later we are, too.

Our buttocks on the kitchen tile are cold, but the passion just above runs white-hot.

"Let's do it," she screams out in the middle of it, loud enough for the Halloweeners on the street to hear. "Take me now, you fuck," she seethes at me, she coos. "Take me for America, give me your baby. Oh, I love you," she says, and she calls out my name. Moments later, the doorbell moans with concerned people on our front doorstep, bothered by the commotion, and we just let it go, and then my own moan rises up, right on pitch and full of life, to meet it.

TOMORROWLAND

There are no bomb shelters or whites-only drinking fountains, but there are plenty of Eisenhower-era comforts of the future: a kitchen of gunmetal appliances in rounded art deco shapes where the wife of the future will enjoy *all manner of convenience* while cooking for man and family. Dinners will be done in minutes instead of hours! Housewives of the future, you will have free time like never before! Imagine a kitchen where dinner cooks itself!

He is old enough to remember this kitsch from the first time around, from before it was kitsch. When it was what people thought would happen. He can remember his father taking him to a showroom once on a Florida family vacation full of long silences—he must've been eight or nine, which would've made the year nineteen fifty-late—an exhibit full of "cars" of the future: flimsy Plexiglas models of T-shaped rockets with wheels hammered on and large glass domes on top. ("Hey Jimmy," his usually-stony father kept saying, pointing to another absurd rocket-car. "Take a look at that one!") Like the vehicles in Commander

Rick Rocket's Saturday-morning serials, which he hadn't thought of in years: how every week, Rick Rocket was left dangling in some impossible cliffhanger, no way the he could survive this time, yet next Saturday he was always back, handsome and serious-minded as ever. Everything was going to be better in the future, where your heroes couldn't be killed. James can still recall how excited it made him as a child, back in that simpler time, imagining what life would be like far in the future, in this time. How he couldn't wait to grow up.

How foolish he was.

A mannequin wife stands in the kitchen. She doesn't smile or reveal emotion because there's nothing in that doll's chest of hers, no heart there. Nothing going on in that molded plastic head, but for just a moment, James thinks she's looking right at him.

She's dressed in a blue-and-white checkered summer dress with a frilly, almost pin-up-girl apron on top. Bent slightly at the waist, leaning toward the imposing stove of the future, her right arm crooked like a Barbie's at a constant thirty-degree angle, reaching ever toward the oven of the future, to take out food of the future, to feed her family of the future. A mitt on her right hand that looks like it's never come off. Red patent leather heels, fake diamond earbobs, a string of faux pearls around her neck. A burnished wedding ring on the hand down by her side. Neither the ring, nor the arm, nor the slender swanlike neck, not her blushing cheek nor the tousle of blonde hair in that perfect '50s style, has felt a human touch in years.

"Look at all this junk," Carlos whines as he comes through the door. He's got a handkerchief to his nose, though they've both got dustmasks hanging around their necks, but it really isn't that bad. Just a closed-off, musty smell, a little like disturbing a crypt.

"Beware the curse," James says to himself, "of Rick Rocket's tomb."

Carlos looks at him confused. "Huh?"

Everything else they'd been to that afternoon—the *Atomic Blast!* coaster, the *Twirling Dimensions!* ride, the hall of mirrors (*Transform Into An Alien!*)—had been desecrated going back years, with graffiti and sets of coupled initials plus 4 Ever, the floors littered in cigarette butts and crushed beer cans, the gates around the rides kicked down and broken, the mirrors in the hall busted out. No respect, James thought when he saw it, bothered by the thought that there were kids out there who'd kick a funhouse mirror for the satisfaction of watching it break. But the Home of the Future had been boarded up tight, like it'd been designed to withstand a war. It took him and Carlos forever to pry their way through the thick boards, and when they finally stepped inside, they found themselves in a past that'd been perfectly preserved.

"Hey, looky here," Carlos calls out, having spotted the mannequin wife. "It's the blow-up doll of the future."

"How about a little respect?" James says sharply—and there's that pesky word again—but then he feels foolish. The mannequin's surely not going to be offended, though she might be disappointed to find men's manners in the 21st century so unimproved. Or maybe she wouldn't be surprised at all.

Carlos doesn't catch the mistake; he's breathed in a whiff of dust and has begun to honk into his handkerchief. It's getting to James too, making him a little misty-eyed—the old air floating with particles. That must be it. Truth be told, he was happy to find the place in such good shape. It was like the fairy tale of the beautiful dead woman buried in the airtight glass case, preserving her splendor, though when he and Carlos had broken in, they hadn't spoiled what was inside, like happens in the story.

At least not yet. But soon.

They've come to tear the place down.

Carlos honks again into the handkerchief. Then he points his gloved finger in the direction of the wife.

"You've really let the place go, baby," he says.

IN THE NEXT PART of the house, the kids are having the time of their lives in the family room of the future: A rounded television on fat legs like a hippo, radio console in the back corner of the room which doubles as a piece of stylish wood-like furniture. Beside the radio sits dad's comfy chair, which has all the amenities you'd expect to find: Press a button and the chair eases dad back after a hard day at the office. Press another and the chair massages and works out the strain in his back, with much the same touch as the wife used to have, before the kids came along, and the upgraded kitchen. The recliner's armrest opens to find an elegant storage space, perfect for dad's pipe, which James can tell is the case because the flip-door is open, and there's a pipe poking out. The Dad himself is nowhere to be seen, but Billy and Suzy don't seem to mind; the mannequin kids are sitting in front of the television, struck dumb by all their good fortune, the boy in a dark blue ballcap with no team affiliation, the girl in a frilly pink dress and string of plastic pearls like her mother. The screen of the television a black cardboard square, with the fake children staring at nothing for years on end, like actual children. Hopefully there's been no atomic explosion in the neighborhood, knocking out the reception.

"Ha," James says.

The pried-off front door only half-lights the room; James runs his flashlight around. The chunky plastic buttons on the armchair glint like hard candy as he sweeps past.

Carlos walks over to the far wall and runs his glove along, as if trying to mind-read. "Asbestos in here I bet. I hate these old houses." Then he seems to catch whatever wistful look is on James's face. "Hey, Jim. You look like you're having a personal moment over there."

James smiles and waves him off. "No, no," he says. "Nothing really."

But Carlos realizes he's hit on something. "C'mon, now. What is it?"

James has never much cared for working with Carlos. Twenty-two and a father twice over already, just a brash kid who laughs too loudly at his own jokes and has that way of putting you down with a wink-nudge, like he doesn't really believe the terrible thing he just said. Not meanness in him, exactly. Hard to say where it comes from, except that young people aren't what they used to be. In the months leading up to what should've been James's retirement, Carlos gave it to him good every day: old man jokes, moving-slow jokes, foot-in-grave jokes. Then James didn't retire. He'd gone into Roger Hamby's office with his hands folded in front of him like a kid in trouble, which is how he felt, and told Roger about Marilyn. How at first, it seemed like a bug, like something she'd come down with. Fever and stomach upset, nothing too worrisome. Then his wife began dropping weight. After three days of bedrest, with James still thinking they were dealing with a virus, Marilyn looked over at him and said calmly, but very sure, "Something's wrong."

They received a grim diagnosis. Treatments began. Tubes in the arm, tubes to breathe, tubes running everywhere. It seemed the machines were sucking out life instead of putting it back in; each day when James came home, and thanked the woman from church he'd hired to sit with her, his wife seemed emptier than when he'd left. Suddenly James found himself in the strange position of begging to keep the job he'd finally walked away from, not only for the health insurance but the weekly paycheck. He and Marilyn had lived cautiously enough, forty-five years of funds put away with due diligence, always looking ahead. Now those patiently-kept funds looked done for.

"So you're saying," Roger Hamby said, shifting in his office chair, "you're saying you want to stay with us for . . . ?"

"For good," James said. "I want to come back, to stay."

Roger no doubt planned on hiring someone half James's age and salary soon as he was gone. This hadn't been a family-run business in years, and Roger was no one James knew outside of the office. He was more the kind of boss where you had to remind him the name of your dying wife. It'd never been that kind of just-a-handshake company even when the Crowes owned it, but it was a place that knew you and took care of you, like family. But in the last decade they'd been bought out and Roger had come in representing a parent company with a made-up word for a name, lots of Xs and Zs, like an alien overlord, and suddenly the place had become less like a family and more just a business. Mr. Crowe put stipulations on preserving the old crew as part of the sale, or James might've been out of a job right then, at an unhireable age.

Roger listened to what James said, looking almost unconvinced. He ran a hand around his face like there was a cobweb stuck there. "So you mean," Roger said again, but there was really no way to put it delicately. "You mean you want to stay with us right up until the moment your wife—?"

"Yes," James said, heading him off. "Until she recovers."

So the retirement party and cake, if there'd been such things, were put on ice. No gold watch was presented to him; did places give those anymore? The young men on the job looked down at their feet when James came around, even more than they'd done before. He reminded them of death, and they were far too young and happy and stupid to be thinking about such things. And the razzing from Carlos stopped cold, though the memory of it remained. Just hung there. Memory had begun to play an increasing role in James's life, much to his surprise, likely because looking behind, for the first time he could think of, seemed a better idea than looking ahead.

Carlos is still waiting for James to answer. He's already got a smirk on his face, in anticipation of whatever this is going to be.

"I remember all this from when I was a kid," James answers

finally, shrugging. "Just the style of it, I guess, and the idea of it. How everybody thought this was how we'd all live by now. So that's it. Just this well-meant optimism that's got me thinking of the past."

"But this *ain't* the past," Carlos corrects him, needling. "This here's the home of the future. Look, the kids even got themselves a big TV. With *cathode tubes* in it. The good life, ain't it? Beautiful wife, two perfect kids, perfect house, no worries."

"Yes," James says, soft.

"Hardly *gets* much better, right?"

James starts to open his mouth, as if there's something he'd like to add or amend. But then he doesn't say anything.

Carlos honks into the handkerchief again, folds it in half and reaches it around, wipes the back of his neck. He removes his hardhat and wipes his forehead, folds the hanky up some more.

"Bet they got a Mexican maid somewheres," he says.

THERE IS NO TOILET in the bathroom of the future.

There's a spacious standup shower rockfaced in artificial river stones, with round hubcap-like discs for showerheads that could've come from a UFO creature feature. His and hers matching sinks, mirrors. Tesla-looking light bulbs like thought bubbles. Two feet of fake marble counterspace between the sinks. Enough distance, you'd never even have to touch.

James and Carlos run their flashlights across it all. It shines back dimly in the dusted mirrors, frosts the porcelain and glass and chrome.

Carlos whistles like he's impressed, though it's hard to know if it's for real.

Further down the darkened hallway they find the children's room: Bunk beds like silver pneumatic tubes, like torpedo bays, as if the children might be launched into space at any moment. Some toys of the future—a baseball, a babydoll, a ray gun. A toychest full of plastic and plush. A robot dog in the middle of the room that catches Carlos off guard and makes him scream out. He takes his foot and pushes it over for revenge. "Dumb mutt."

Baseball pennants of teams called Martians and Venusians over the boy's bunk.

A small American flag, faded.

"Wonder if this stuff's valuable?" Carlos asks. He puts his flashlight between jaw and shoulder and kneels down in front of the toychest, rooting around and making a mess. Might as well; it's all going to be discarded anyway. "Maybe my kids'll want some of this crap."

Then the walkies beep in unison, a perfect robot noise—it's Roger, wondering where they are. Carlos drops the toys and answers off-speaker, holding it to his ear with his shoulder. "Naw boss, we're good. Making one last walkthrough. It can come down today. Some stuff in here to toss is all." When he's finished, he clips the walkie back to his belt, then wheels around and makes for James with the ray gun in his hand, pulls the trigger. But there's no light show, no alien sound effect. Long dead. Just an unfulfilling click.

THERE IS ONE ROOM LEFT—the bedroom of the future. For some reason the doorway is sealed in plastic; James's flashlight sends back a dull circle reflected off. He walks the hallway down, flashlight bobbing, pokes at the plastic with his finger, taut. Then he takes out his pocketknife and slices down the middle of the sheet, and the room sighs. He feels a brief hesitation—like grave robbing, he thinks, or the calm beat in a monster movie before the thing jumps out and scares the audience. He puts his arm through the plastic, almost to test the other side, and pokes his whole body through.

This is where the Dad has been hiding.

Two well-made beds, his and hers, like on *I Love Lucy*. Dad is sitting on the edge of the closest one, propped forward uncomfortably with his hands resting on his knees. Dressed in a slim brown suit from an ancient Sears catalogue, square hanky in the breast pocket, the suitcoat rumpled with age. He is wearing a jetpack. There's a fishbowl on his head and a far-off look on his face, staring straight down at the floor like the last shocked survivor of some space calamity. (James gave a start when the flashlight passed him, had to catch his breath.)

It makes sense, on a reptile-brain level, that this room would have the weirdest feel: it's the darkest, the farthest back, then there's the fact that it'd been sealed off like that, the plastic hanging from the doorframe now like split flesh. Something about it prickles James's armhairs as he steps further inside and scans the flashlight around: '50s-era dresser and bureau in cobwebs. A clouded mirror. Wires drooping from the ceiling and thick dust on the floor that he disturbs with his bootsteps, sending it rolling into the air like smoke. One of the wires hanging from the ceiling brushes the top of James's head like a finger. He's never been one to spook easily, and in his long working life he'd been through many haunted old places, but something about this room feels very off . . . it's the same thing, he realizes, that keeps attracting the beam of his flashlight. It's the Dad in that slumped-over position, that strange expression on his face. Not the wax-museum fear that the Dad might lift his eyes up at James, which he'd almost felt would happen in the kitchen, with the mannequin wife. Strangely, it's almost the fact that the Dad does not look at him. There's the sense he could do just that, at any moment, but instead his head is hung down as if he's been caught at something.

"Hey *Jim*," Carlos calls out from the kids' room. "You find anything?"

But James can't shake the expression on the mannequin. That's just the expression he came with, of course, the one someone decided to fix on him back then, right for the time period; could you imagine some Cold War department-store male mannequin with a broad smile on its face? Smiling about what? Red Menace? Nuclear annihilation? The Negro Problem? The Korean Peninsula? These are the faces they had on back then, James reminds himself: the stoic father, the accommodating mother, the fascinated children. The whole culture wore those faces, for a long time.

Besides, what would the Dad of the future have to be upset about? He's got it all right in front of him, with the touch of a button. He works in outer space or something, might even be a kind of super-spy. His wife is beautiful and submissive. His kids are self-entertained. The

Dad of the future has it all, just like Carlos said. He's got the world in his hands. He could just have a martini from the Instashaker Cocktail Machine and loosen the hell up.

But then there's that look on him. That slight slump forward.

It's the breaking of the illusion that has James so ill at ease. Not the same expression as the wife or children, the fantasy of the perfect life, but a look that feels heavier and therefore real. In a home of molded plastic faces, it strikes him as the first human expression James has seen.

He won't even look you in the face.

This is the reason, perhaps, that the wife is on the other side of the house, striking her pose in the kitchen, pretending that everything is fine. Why the kids are in front of the tube, entertaining themselves.

Everyone in the house of the future knows: there's something wrong with Dad.

You two go watch television, your father is sick.

But I want to see Daddy.

Don't you go back there. Your father is sick.

But sick with what? James wonders. Is there even a name for what the Dad's feeling way back then? Is there a name for it now? How he did everything right by the book, worked hard, never missed a space-day of his space-job, met and married his beautiful wife, built the home of the future with everything in its right place . . . yet in the mornings the Dad stares at his face in the mirror and thinks to himself, and surprises himself by thinking it, *Something's wrong.* This is not what it was supposed to be. (*Something's wrong,* Marilyn said matter-of-factly.) The Dad has figured out what James has figured out: how none of this is real. This dream of a perfect future. The thought that, if you could just survive long enough, all of your problems would be solved.

Just then a terrible thought occurs to James: Dad's air. It can't possibly be on. James doesn't hear that hiss of oxygen he's now too-familiar with, and why would the Dad be wearing the helmet inside, anyway? Are we not on Earth? Why would he be the only one wearing it, not the others? Why is he back here alone?

The expression and dread mood of the room suddenly make sense to him.

The Dad is asphyxiating himself.

He's put on the airtight helmet and not turned the valve. Put the helmet on and sealed it, sat down with his hands on his knees thinking, *Can I do this?* In a moment the fishbowl will fog with breath, then the glass will go clear, and it will be done. *And for what?* everyone will say after, at the HOA meetings of the future or at bridge clubs. *What was so wrong with his life,* they'll ask over martinis, *that he had to throw it all away?*

"Hey, Jim, what's back there?"

Suddenly James is ashamed of himself for what he's thinking, for his cynicism. There are times when his own mood gets as heavy and sinks as still and solemn as the dummy's in front of him, but it's in those moments that Marilyn, the one slipping away, is there to comfort him. "It'll be all right," she says, reading him correctly, stroking his hand lightly with her fingertips, using the future tense, *It will.* Marilyn tells him this often, and she'll tell him again tonight when he returns home as exhausted by worry as work, and James will choose to believe her when she says it, because he must.

Maybe, James thinks, this is what the Dad needs to hear, too. He's been locked in this dark place, with his dark thoughts, for so long that he needs someone to tell him it's okay, even if it's a lie. Maybe all he needs is a hand—if James approached the Dad and touched him on the shoulder, gave him a slight push. Lifted him back up. But he's missed his chance; Carlos is stomping down the hallway, making an awful racket with his armful of vintage toys, flashlight tucked under his elbow sending frantic searchlights with each step.

He punches his head through the plastic and looks around.

"Fucking creepy," he says.

"Yes," James says, lowering the light from the Dad's face. "It is."

"Roger wants us out. Go take a look at the lovers' boatride so they can bring in the dozers. Rocket Man's getting smushed."

James turns to look at the Dad one last time and thinks of telling him, in fact almost does, *It'll be all right, old man.* But he doesn't. Not because Carlos would think he's lost it, but because he already knows what's in store for this family: that there's a force with the sole purpose of knocking them down on its way, and they just don't know it yet. But that's probably the way it ought to be, James thinks. If you knew for a fact what the future held, who'd ever have the courage to face it? Instead, he reaches out and raises the mannequin up to a better posture, tilts the fishbowl slightly so that the Dad is sitting straight, looking up confidently, and he tells him simply, "Best of luck," which he means earnestly, and means for them both. For them all. It's the only thing he can do. Then he turns and follows Carlos out of the bedroom and back up the black hallway, through the family room and past the stunned kids, past the beautiful mannequin wife standing in the kitchen, then he is out the front door and blinded by sunlight, blinking ghosts in his eyes, reemerging with difficulty into the already-vanishing present moment of this unreal life.

BOARDWALK ELVIS

Boardwalk Elvis walked and chafed. He strutted the boardwalk and swiveled his hips and made Elvis noises to himself, and when the mood hit him he stopped and struck a pose—the Aloha From Hawaii, the Jailhouse Rock, the Too Much Bacon. He passed an elderly couple holding hands and spoke politely, but neither made eye contact with him. He passed through a group of Jehovah's Witnesses and came out the other side with some literature. He intersected a round of shaggy hippies playing hackysack and returned one of their volleys off the side of the pier.

It was Memorial Day weekend, the second-best weekend of the entire summer for boardwalk Elvising. Vendors with cotton candy and caramel apples lined the pier, stands with seven-dollar cokes and five-dollar hot dogs; flocks of zincnosed out-of-towners milled around who might get a charge from meeting a boardwalk Elvis. Barechested college boys bullied their way around the promenade, high school kids gossiped and dove in and out of video arcades. Bikini girls skated by and smiled, bursting from red, white, and blue scraps, and Boardwalk raised an index finger.

"Girls," he said, and he pointed the finger like a gun.

He passed a twenty-something mother in a sundress bent down to her child.

"Look," the mother said, pointing at him. "Do you know who that is?"

"Elvis," the little girl said.

"Do you want to take a picture with him?"

"No."

"Hey there, little lady," Boardwalk said, sauntering up to her. "Wanna get a photo with Boardwalk E?"

The little girl bit her cheek and shook her head as if refusing medicine.

"Come on," the mother said, fishing through her oversized purse for her camera. "I want to get one."

Boardwalk Elvis knelt down.

"Come on, little lady," he said, reaching for her.

The girl moved stiffly, arms straight down by her sides, and positioned herself beside his jumpsuit-stench. She wrinkled her nose.

"Get closer," the mother said, gesturing. "Put your arm around him."

"Let me be your teddy bear," Boardwalk said.

She did as she was told and put a cautious arm on his back.

"Now smile!"

Boardwalk Elvis put a hand in the air, forking finger and thumb in the Hawaiian handsign for love. The little girl squinted and snarled.

"That's perfect," said the mother, snapping the picture. "That's going to be great."

"Glad I could help you, ma'am," Boardwalk answered in his exaggerated Tupelo drawl, rising to his feet. The girl ran to her mother's side.

"She acts the same way with Santa Claus."

"I like Santa's style. Both Santa and the Boardwalk E want to bring smiles to little snaggletooth faces."

"That's great," the mother said, shuffling her camera back into her purse. "Thank you so much."

"That'll be five dollars," said Boardwalk.

"Oh," blushed the mother, rummaging her purse for money. "All I have is a ten."

"Thank you, thank you very much."

BOARDWALK E STROLLED through the crowds on the pier and slurped at a snow cone. He could feel a rash starting under his jumpsuit. It was an occupational hazard and happened every year, beginning as an itch on Spring Break and starting to irritate him by Memorial Day. After this, when June was here, the vacationers would become more insistent, as would the spread of rash, and by July 4th the spread would be almost unbearable . . . but he'd be at the top of his game, the hottest sequined property on the boardwalk.

"*Sufferin for muh art,*" he said to himself, nodding his head.

Business had been good most of the morning. He'd taken six pictures for a total loot of forty-two dollars—two with children, two with adults, two with drunk rednecks. And he'd made three dollars by singing "Hound Dog" to a family's cocker spaniel, which licked its balls throughout the performance. But money wasn't the important thing; he would do it for free, he always said, which was mostly what happened. He was an artist, his canvas himself, his strut, his sneer, his pelvis, and artists weren't in it for the money, they were in it for the *high*. There were plenty of street performers on the boardwalk—a juggler or two, a gang of whiteface mimes that roamed around pretending to tug ropes or open doors, every so often a granola with a guitar—and surely their dreams were no more foolish-looking than his.

Boardwalk E walked past a group of high school kids, boys in oversized jeans which barely hung onto their butts and girls in cutoffs and bikini tops. They'd been talking loudly, sharing cigarettes, laughing and cursing, until they saw him.

"Say, how's it goin'?" Boardwalk asked as he passed.

"Shut up, dickhead," laughed one of the boys.

Boardwalk stopped.

The one who spoke—a bucktooth-looking bastard with a beard scraggly and pubic—muttered something under his breath that sounded like *homo*, and the other kids, the girls in particular, laughed.

"I'm sorry," Boardwalk twanged. "What did you say?"

"Nothing, dickhead." The girls laughed again, raised white-filtered cigarettes to their lips between glittered fingernails.

"Say there," Boardwalk said, "that's really no way to speak to your elders, son."

"I'm not your son, dickhead," the bucktooth said.

"He's not your son, dickhead," said the fat kid beside him.

Boardwalk sighed and stepped closer. The kids raised from their slouches and squared their shoulders for a rumble, like maybe they'd seen in the movies.

"Look, kids, there's no need to get rude. We all want to have a good time here."

"Why don't you get your rocks off somewhere else?" the first boy said.

"Now wait just a minute."

"Yeah, can't you get your rocks off somewhere else, dickhead?" the fat boy repeated.

"Now wait just a minute."

"You smell bad," said one of the girls.

"Thank you very much," Boardwalk Elvis said, and walked on.

HE'D BECOME ACCUSTOMED to humiliation over the years and generally took it in stride. A shop owner once turned a hose on him for standing in front of the man's emporium of cheap, breakable crap. Another time, he'd happened upon a beach party thrown by a local politician for kids with prosthetic limbs, complete with Nerf Tetherball and a camera crew. He'd barely bitten into his first hotdog when the politician's goons roughed him up and threw his lunch in the sand. Not everyone got him, and not everyone cared. This was just the risk of doing something bold.

He remembered hearing that the first time Elvis played the Grand Ole Opry he was told he should go back to driving a truck, and the first time he played Vegas, in 1956, the bluehairs in the audience booed. He thought there must be a thousand stories like this, stories of struggle and artists failing, maybe even people like Mozart, and he thought he'd have to check that out one day. But the point of the story seemed to be that sometimes the audience wouldn't know real, legendary, awesome talent if it swiveled its hips suggestively at them. For this reason he'd always taken his rejections well, as the kind of necessary tension that makes the pearl, and had long ago come to peace with the notion that being an artist occasionally meant making oneself look like a fool.

So he walked the pier end to end, making friends and influencing people. The heat bore down on him, reflecting off the white of his jumpsuit and storing in the black of his massive pompadour wig. Soon he was wet with sweat, but still he kept on, strutting along and muttering to himself about *sufferin* and *sac-ruh-fice*. A few people heard him talking to himself and turned to stare, and he shot them the finger-gun in response.

He stopped in front of a group of college girls in thong bikinis, standing around the pier and letting people watch them.

"Say there, little ladies," Boardwalk said.

He got in his judo stance and did some quick jabbing and stabbing into the air.

One of the girls rolled her eyes.

"I'm the Boardwalk Elvis," Boardwalk Elvis said. "I'm a hunka burnin' love."

He fluttered his arms and went down on one knee into what he thought of as Falcon pose.

"No thank you," one of the girls said.

"No thank you to what?" he asked.

One girl put her cell phone to her ear and pretended to talk.

"Aren't you burning up in that?" asked the tallest girl, a thin redhead with death-pale skin who looked like she needed more SPF.

"It's a little warm in here," Boardwalk answered, standing up straight, slightly out of breath. The sweat on his jowls had begun to loosen the adhesive on his muttonchops, so he slid them back in place. "But the heat's a small price to pay for entertaining you lovely ladies."

The brunette with the pug face and the cell phone sighed. "Not that easily entertained, dude," she said.

"Thank you very much," he said.

His WIFE HAD WARNED HIM that morning to take it easy. Forecasters were calling for a scorcher, highs pushing ninety-seven, unseasonable for this time of year, and unreasonable for Elvising at any time, as polyester was not a fabric that breathed. She'd woken up early and put out his jumpsuit for him, along with a few dollars she had on her for water. By the time Boardwalk began to suit up, Marsha was dressed in her neat nursing scrubs, ready to leave for work. They stood together in the bathroom using the mirror, she fixing her sparse makeup and he applying the muttonchops.

"Really," she said. "We're going to be slammed all day with people who overdid it. This heat's going to catch people off guard. Make sure you're not one of them, okay?"

"You know it, *mamacita*," he said, trying on the voice as he applied the sideburn. Then he dropped the voice and said, "Yeah, I will."

The first time they met, he was Elvis at a supermarket. Nothing promotional; he was just shopping. She'd paid for two of his items when the twelve-items-or-less woman gave him grief for fourteen. One of them was a bottle of wine. They drank it at her place, and in the morning he deliberately left his pompadour so he could see her again. He'd sung songs about love at first sight for as long as he'd been an Elvis—though he'd sung many more about heartbreak—but he'd never actually experienced anything close to that kind of feeling in real life. Not many women had ever taken him that seriously. He came with some baggage. But the connection he felt with Marsha was true and immediate. He took her out to eat, dressed as himself, and took her out again dressed as the Boardwalk Elvis, and she seemed as comfortable in his presence both ways. Not the least bit embarrassed. It wasn't that she was the only person who fully understood him—she didn't entirely and made no secret of it, and furthermore she cared more for the Godfather of Soul than for the King—but from the beginning she'd accepted him for what he did, or for what he was, if there was a difference between the two. She accepted him so fully, in fact, that he began to suspect she was pulling some sort of scam on him. So he asked, point blank, what it was she saw in him, or more to the point, how it was that being seen with him in public didn't shame her. He'd assumed that any woman he ended up with would, at the very least, feel a little funny to be out with him when he was in character.

But she gave it to him straight: she'd had a number of relationships with normal-seeming guys who were in truth violent-tempered, controlling, not physically cruel but emotionally for sure. They dressed in regular clothes and went to regular jobs, and the two of them together looked like they led happy, secure lives, and it was all an act. "You're different from that," she said, building to her answer, and when he got sheepish and tried to play this off—I'm sure different, ha ha—she'd have none of it. "You are," she said. "And it's not the outfit. Though that's weird, sure. But you've got this kind of innocence about you that lets you go out like that. You don't have a malicious bone in your body. Your heart is a little funnier than most, I'll give you that, but your heart is true."

She brought him to meet her parents just after he proposed, and he dressed in slacks and a button-up, on his best behavior. But the grace barely hit the amen when her father asked, So what do you do for a living? At the time he was a telemarketer and said so, but her father narrowed his eyes and said, You know what I mean. So he offered a broad explanation of Elvising: you put on an Elvis costume and walk around, maybe sing "Hawaiian Love Song" at a few weddings. He said it was a form of art, like acting or interpretive dance. He said nobody really *chooses* their dream, right? It kind of chooses them, right? Her father got drunk on Jack Daniel's and started calling Marsha's high school boyfriends on the phone. Her mother locked herself in the bathroom and made inhuman moaning sounds. It looked dire.

But Marsha defended him and stood her ground, sobered her father up and calmed her mother down, and over the years his relationship with her parents had mellowed into something like cordiality. He went fishing with her father just last summer, in fact, taking time off from the boardwalk to accept the invitation, and the only sharp thing that passed between the two of them for the entire weekend was a hook.

Nevertheless, he understood where her parents were coming from—it was not just the getup or the strange behavior, but the fact that half his year was spent Elvising rather than pursuing what might be called a career, and Marsha took on the household burdens to let him do it. This had never caused any rift between him and his wife, because she wasn't like that, but certainly it crossed his mind from time to time. How could it not? Like he was a struggling actor or writer or painter, though an actor or writer or painter might at least have something to show for the effort—a fast-food commercial audition, or a manuscript people could pass around, or a watercolor. His goals were a little harder to define, a little harder to measure, and even when opportunities arose for him to perform his art in front of an audience that was open to it, he didn't always come away with anything demonstrable in terms of success, like the competition he'd entered several years ago at Graceland, Show Us Your King, where he'd gone onstage and done his best poses and placed 16th behind a Black Elvis, Italian Elvis, Little Person Elvis, Lady Elvis, Tolkien Middle Earth Elvis, and a couple of Elvises who didn't even look to be trying. At the end of the day he was given the same small plastic trophy as everyone who'd paid the entry fee. That was a long drive home, Marsha behind the wheel almost the whole way, while he sat in the passenger's seat with his face against the cool window. The only words she offered about it came just after they got to the car, still in the Graceland parking lot: "I thought you did great."

He was tightening his oversized belt when she came in to kiss him goodbye. The suit wasn't quite right—he'd gained a little around the middle since the previous season, and he was having trouble getting the zipperseam to sit right.

"I'll come out and see you in a few days," she said, and leaned forward to kiss him on the cheek.

Watching the kiss in the mirror, she so reasonable and smart in her uniform, he so obviously not, he felt a twinge of familiar guilt.

"Do you ever wish I'd grow up?" he asked.

"No, I like the child I married," she said.

He watched as she smoothed the front of his jumpsuit.

"Gonna be late," she said with a pat of his belly. "Do us proud."

Then she went out toward the door of their apartment in a rush, jangling her car keys. The last thing she called out was, "And please, please remember to be careful."

"Don't you worry about me, little lady," he called back in character, practice-snarling his lip in the bathroom mirror. "What could possibly go wrong?"

By four o'clock, Boardwalk Elvis was close to heatstroke. His head was heavy but drifted, like an anvil floating on a balloon string. He could feel his blood pressure beating in his eyes. Tourists continued to approach him for pictures, but the last few had also asked if he was feeling okay.

"It's the heat," Boardwalk said. "Not to worry, though. Boardwalk E is fine. Heat ain't nothing but a bunny in traffic."

The tourists said, Excuse me?

"A traffic bunny," Boardwalk repeated, a little louder. "Not the band Traffic, though they did have some fine songs."

Boardwalk realized he wasn't faking it well when he staggered into a hot dog vendor and took down a stack of red-and-white Coca-Cola cups. He apologized and said it was polyester don't breathe. Havin trouble.

The vendor filled a cup with ice water.

"Take this and sit down and sip it," the man said. "And if you feel dizzy like you're about to die, don't do it here."

Boardwalk staggered to the strip where the restaurants and small shops selling Formosa Beach half-shirts were and sat down close to a store wall, where at least a moderate shade hit the ground, the stone pleasantly cool on his wig and slick back. He wouldn't mind if any of the shop owners came out and hosed him off today.

He sipped the ice water slowly, his heartrate beginning to calm, and watched the families and the kids pass him slowly on their way nowhere in flip-flopping strides. Sweat rolled into his eyes and settled in, stinging. He took off his oversized sunglasses and wiped his face with his sleeve.

When he opened his eyes again, Boardwalk Elvis saw a little boy with an ice-cream cone standing over him, staring down.

"Are you alive?" the boy asked.

"Most definitely, little fella," Boardwalk said. His mouth almost stuck shut. He sipped his water.

"I thought you might be dead."

"Well, then, thanks for checking up. But I'm still alive."

"I've never seen a dead body before," the boy said.

"Me neither."

The boy licked his cone, sending a line of drool and vanilla down his chin and onto his shirt. He looked to be nine or ten, Boardwalk thought, but he wasn't sure. He had a close summer haircut and was missing a tooth.

Boardwalk rose to his feet slowly, swaying like a gaudy oak.

"Are you here on vacation, little fella?"

"Are you a superhero?" the boy asked, ignoring the question.

"No, no," Boardwalk said, trying to get back into character. "I'm Boardwalk Elvis."

"What the hell is that?" the boy asked.

"I'm an Elvis that comes down to the boardwalk."

"Why?"

"To bring snaggletooth grins to kids and stuff, like you." He rubbed the frosty, water-beaded cup across his face.

"You're not a superhero?"

"I hate to tell you this," Boardwalk E said, "but superheroes don't exist."

"Neither does Elvis," the boy answered. "He's dead."

Boardwalk took turns sipping from his water and rubbing the cup across his cheeks and forehead. The boy watched, not speaking, waiting for a reply.

"Well yes," Boardwalk said finally, sliding his shades back on, "but as long as the music lives, then so will the King. So okay. Time to move on now, I guess." He checked the wristwatch he wasn't wearing.

"So what do you do?" asked the boy. "Where's your guitar?"

"I don't bring it anymore. My fingers get too sweaty to play."

This was a lie. He didn't own a guitar.

"Does someone pay you to come out here dressed like that?"

"No."

"Nobody pays you?"

"No," he sighed. "Nobody pays the Boardwalk E. Unless you want to take a picture with me."

"Nope," the boy said. "So if you don't get paid, and if you're not a superhero, then why do you dress up like that and walk around?"

"You ask a lot of questions," Boardwalk Elvis said. "Don't you have somewhere you have to be?"

"I do not."

The boy dribbled more ice cream onto his shirt.

"How do you make a living?" the kid asked.

"How do you make a living?" Boardwalk snapped back.

"I'm just a kid, I don't have to."

"My wife works," he said, suddenly very disinterested in this conversation.

"Your wife works?"

"Yes."

"So you can dress like Elvis and walk around in the sun?"

"Yes."

"You're a butthole," the boy grinned. "Your wife should leave you."

"Fuck off, kid."

"Johnny," called a woman from several stores down. "Come on, let's go eat."

"That cone's gonna totally ruin your appetite," Boardwalk warned.

"That's my mom," the boy said. "She's married to a bum, too."

For a moment he had the urge to grab the little bastard by his neck and squeeze, just lift him off the ground and shake him until his eyes bugged out, but the boy had already turned and started to walk toward his mother. Then when he got a few feet away, the boy turned and walked back, as if he'd reconsidered the conversation and had something to add.

"You really oughtta be a superhero or something useful," the kid said. "Use your suit as a force of good. At least then you'd have a reason to walk around dressed like such a butthole all the time."

Boardwalk watched as the kid shuffled back into the loping crowd. He sat back down and finished up his cup of water and kept looking back in the kid's direction, as if he expected him to come back for one more round of insults.

Shortly thereafter, he decided he needed something stronger to drink.

BANANAS LOUNGE was right on the strip, a frequent end-of-the-day stop where old men drank in silence while their wives walked the pier and wobbled. It was the last place in town where you could smoke inside, and for that reason it was almost always empty, regardless of how many people were still walking around outside. Most of the regular clientele looked to be waiting for death. The peanuts were old, the jukebox was country.

"Frank," Boardwalk said, "hit me again."

"No one actually says that," said Frank the bartender.

"What do they say?"

"They say, 'May I have another?' Guys who come in here all important and say hit me, I usually do."

Frank put another drink in front of him. Boardwalk stuck his hand into the back pocket he'd sewn on the jumpsuit himself and handed the bartender a crumpled five. He'd been bellied up for an hour already, he thought, or possibly two. He drank bourbon after bourbon and told Frank everything.

"This has been a really shitty day," he said, beginning to slur his words. "I tell you, between the sun and all those bastards running around out there . . . "

"You still mad at that kid?"

"Damn right."

"I've often wondered myself why you walk around like that," Frank said.

"I do it for the fans," Boardwalk said.

Frank the bartender lit a cigarette.

"Sounds like the fans really appreciate it," Frank said, and exhaled.

From the front window the sun had set, or was in the process of it, burning the faces that passed a bright orange. The lights on the pier had begun to twinkle on.

"Look, what do you expect from people, when you go out dressed like that?"

"I don't know," Boardwalk said. "Snaggletoothed smiles? At least a good time."

"For them, or for you?"

"I don't see why that matters," Boardwalk said. "I don't see why both ain't possible."

"Or neither."

Boardwalk missed his mouth with his bourbon. He picked up a napkin and wiped his face.

"I do it for the fans. For the ones who really get it, anyway. The rest of them can kiss it."

"Hey, did you see any of that game today? Motherfucking O's blew another one. I don't know what they're doing with all that payroll, but they're not putting it on the field."

"But the fans *do* appreciate it," Boardwalk said. "There's a bunch who appreciate it. Otherwise I'd hang it up after all these years."

"It's that bullpen," Frank said, shaking his head.

"Yes, I do it for the fans, that's what it all comes down to," Boardwalk Elvis said. "An artist ain't nothing without an audience, you know."

"Is that true?" Frank asked.

But Boardwalk had to think about it. He remembered the story of the bluehairs booing.

"Okay, so you can't always listen to the audience," Boardwalk said. "They can't always be trusted to know what's what."

"That's good for you, then," Frank said. "Because nobody around here understands you. Nobody knows what the fuck you think you're doing is what I mean. Maybe some really like what you do, but all I ever hear is how people think you're a retard." Frank reached under the bar and produced a wooden bowl. "Peanuts?"

Boardwalk Elvis put down his drink.

"What?" he asked, leaning in. "What did you just say?"

"People think you're retarded," Frank repeated. Then he corrected himself. "Sorry, I mean *challenged*. They think you're one of these people who get jobs at McDonald's under their let-a-retard-get-your-fries program. Sorry, I mean challenged."

"What?"

"I saw that game," said the only other patron at the bar, an old man with a face that was wrinkled and jowled like a scrotum. "Worst damn bullpen out there if you ask me, excuse my French. And that's a shame, because I've been an O's fan for many years."

"Hold on a second," Boardwalk Elvis said, interrupting. "Go

back to what you were saying before."

"It's the pitching," Frank repeated.

"No, about what people think of me."

"I shouldn't have said anything," the bartender conceded. "Just forget it. I didn't mean it. Even if I did, it's not my business. I'm a live-and-let-live guy. Just let it wash over you, buddy. Say, how about one on the house?"

Frank mixed another drink and put it on the bar.

"But maybe you should think about retiring," said Frank. "Or maybe take a little break, that's all. Give people around here a summer to miss you, see what happens."

"What if they don't miss me?"

"Then you don't want to go where you're not wanted, right? No big deal. Nobody understands you. You don't make any money and it's not making you famous or anything, and you keep on doing it. In fact, you look like it makes you miserable sometimes, but so what? Nobody knows what the fuck you're doing. That's all. It's no big deal." Frank shrugged for emphasis before moving down to the other end of the bar, to resume conversation with the old man about the demise of the Birds.

Boardwalk gulped his bourbon in silence. He felt woozy, the combination of sun and liquor, but the whiskey was smooth and made his stomach and bowels feel pleasantly loose. He'd had bad days before, plenty of them, had a bad year once, a depressing stab at Vegas in his twenties, struggling to stand out against a horde of sequined amateurs on the strip, but there's only so much failure a person can take before the doubt begins to creep in, and by the end of the year he couldn't wait to pack up and head east. He might've given it up then, leaving Las Vegas for Formosa Beach; it might've even been the smart thing to do. But he'd been steadfast despite the setbacks in his belief that he served an important function, bringing the King to the boardwalk's summer days. Then he'd met Marsha and found himself, for the first time, with a support system in place, and that helped keep him going. But Frank had a point—if it wasn't the money and wasn't snaggletoothed smiles, if it couldn't be for the fans because according to his friend the bartender, most everyone thought he was mentally challenged, what was he really hoping for, then?

"I want to matter," Boardwalk said to himself. And he was glad it was to himself, because this was a ridiculous thing to say, even if it was right. He could think back to the feeling that came over him the first time he saw Elvis on stage—watching a taped performance of *Live from Madison Square Garden* on a Sunday afternoon with his mother when he was just a kid, about the age of the kid who game him such grief today. Transfixed, watching the King take command of the stage with that cape around him like Superman. That moment had altered the course of Boardwalk's strange life. There was no explaining a religious experience to anyone, you either felt the light upon you or you didn't, but Boardwalk felt the change in him at that young moment, and he still felt it. That's what he was after, both in the giving and receiving. He wanted to be meaningful. He wanted to matter. And this was the risk he faced in going out every time, the risk of finding out that he did not, in fact, matter a damn.

Boardwalk took one long last sip off his drink, his complimentary one untouched and beading, then rose from his barstool with a bit of struggle.

"Too much money and not enough brains," Frank was preaching across the bar. "Hey, Boardwalk, you out?"

"I don't think I like you anymore," Boardwalk Elvis said.

Both Frank and the old man stopped to look at him.

"Or not right now, anyway," Boardwalk corrected.

With that, he straightened his wig, knocked over his barstool, and stumbled out of the bar into the humid evening.

THE WALK HOME was relatively short. He and Marsha lived five-and-a-half blocks from the boardwalk in a dilapidated building that the City of Formosa Beach wanted to either declare historic or knock down to build condos. He kept his eyes on the sidewalk and walked in drunk strides. The streets in the neighborhood weren't particularly well-lit, though he sure was, but he was able to see the sidewalk from the reflection of the rising moon off his jumpsuit. Once he realized he was wearing his sunglasses, seeing was even easier.

"Retard at McDonald's," he muttered.

He stumbled on a break in the pavement but caught himself from falling; he listened to the irregular sound of his drunk feet on the sidewalk and tried to imagine how he would explain his day to Marsha, who was going to be none-too-pleased to see her husband coming in stewed. He should've peed before he left the bar, he realized sadly. It occurred to him a way to solve the problem might be to duck down one of the side-alleys and urinate in public. This seemed to him an excellent and well-conceived plan, so he took a turn down an alleyway in between buildings after just a block, walking down the alley almost sideways. He found a suitable spot and undid the long zipper—having to unzip his entire torso just to piss—and was comforted by the pleasant steam-sound of his urine on the side of someone's apartment, a loud psshh adding to the share of sounds Formosa Beach always had, like the rough wind coming off the waters, the hiss of tide you could hear blocks back, depending on the time of day, the barely perceivable hum of humid static in the air, and now the warm hiss he added with a pleasant grunt.

But then as the stream went on and on, Boardwalk realized that he heard something else. Some other sound that didn't fit with the rest, coming from the clearing in back of the apartment building, out the other side of the alley. He peed some more and zipped himself up finally and refastened his belt, then he walked back with the noise getting closer, though he couldn't yet tell what it was or who it belonged to. The sounds were almost non-sounds: whimpers, moans and gasps, short, sharp breaths. Copulation sounds, he thought, and a jolt of anticipation went through him. They were coming from the small patch of dirt and crabgrass between two apartment buildings, not a habitable courtyard of any sort, no real direct light source, nowhere people ought to be.

He stopped at the end of the alleyway and cocked his head, strained his eyes toward the clearing. He could see shapes of something, shapes of several somethings, his vision adjusting to the distance and half-darkness. Straining, he could see three people standing almost in a circle, their backs to him, around a person on the ground. A man, it seemed, the source of the distress. The three standing raised their legs and brought their feet down on the prone man's body, neck, and head.

Boardwalk watched for almost a full minute before it registered what was happening. Then he decided that he should get back through the alley, out to the relative safety of the public street, and move the hell on quickly before anyone spotted him. So a guy was getting beat up. That was a shame. People were pretty miserable, which is something he'd figured out even before this capper to an excellent day. But this was not his business, and not his concern.

He'd taken three steps down the alley when he heard the voice of the little shithead from the walk come back to him: *Use that suit for a force of good. At least you'd have a reason to walk around dressed like such a butthole all the time.*

Get out of my mind, little shithead, he tried to think.

He'd barely taken another step when he heard the voice of his wife this time, assuring him, *Your heart is true.*

He knew he should just keep walking, he knew the liquor was doing his thinking for him, and he was more than ready to put this day away forever. But his shifting sense of self, rearranging all day, shifted once again or more accurately stumbled, and before he knew it, without thinking of what he was about to do, the decision had been made.

Boardwalk stopped and turned back toward the scene.

"Hey there," he called out.

The beating stopped mid-beat, legs froze mid-kick. The standing men turned their torsos to face him with their knees cocked in the air. They looked like baffled flamingoes.

"Hey now," Boardwalk repeated, trying to put some gut into it, some gravitas, but he had none left. He raised a pointer finger at them. "What say you leave that little guy alone?"

Boardwalk moved slowly, cautiously, toward them, though his knees were knocking inside his jumpsuit. The attackers stood with their legs still in the air, but it was their faces, their expressions, he noticed as he drew close enough to make them out in the moonlight. Their mouths wide open, their eyebrows up and befuddled, faces crooked in shock.

"Move on now," Boardwalk said.

"What in the fuck is that?" said one of the attackers.

The huddled men put their feet down.

"Is that Elvis?"

"That's right, it's Elvis," Boardwalk Elvis said. "Defender of the Boardwalk who knows judo. So now leave that guy alone or—"

There was silence for a moment that felt longer than a moment but for the breeze from the ocean and the distant quiet crash of tide and his heartbeat going calypso. Then one of the attackers smiled and laughed. Ditto the second, ditto the third, ditto even the guy on the ground.

Boardwalk Elvis was the only one not laughing.

"I'm *serious*," he said, doubling down.

"You look it."

He couldn't see any of their faces too clearly but imagined brutish angles and hard jaws and probably tough-looking scars or something. The three assailants then mumbled something between themselves, something low with menace, and began walking slowly in Boardwalk's direction. They continued to chuckle randomly.

"Good," Boardwalk said, backing up. "I guess you're gonna leave him alone now."

The men continued to advance on him. One cracked his knuckles.

"Okay then," Boardwalk said. "I guess my work here is done."

Now Boardwalk was headed in the direction of home listening to not just his own footfalls but four sets of footfalls, and three of them were getting louder. He took the turn out of the alley so clumsily that he almost wiped out right there, and as soon as he was in straightaway he began flailing his arms as he ran, screaming for help, no longer in a velvet-smooth drawl but in a nasal, high-pitched New Jersey whine.

"Help! Help!" he yelled, though he vaguely remembered something someone told him about yelling "fire" instead of "help" in an emergency, because who in their right mind would help a total stranger?

Running blindly now toward his apartment, running as fast as his suede shoes would take him, three blocks away, then two and a half, when one of the guys landed on his back and sent him plummeting onto the sidewalk in a bellyflop. Immediately there were sneakered feet on him—in his gut, on his back, his face. Finding hollows all over his his body and planting kicks there.

"This is for 'In the Ghetto!'" one of them said, and kicked him in the side of the head, sending his wig flying off.

"No, for 'Suspicious Minds!'" said another, and kicked him thankfully only near the groin.

"Viva Las Vegas!" said the third, *kick*.

Boardwalk felt his consciousness begin to flicker, he heard a ringing in his ears that was almost more of a scream, a twirling, diving noise, and he thought this might be how passing out sounded until one of his attackers said, "C'mon man, cops."

Suddenly the kicks were gone, the laughing gone, but Boardwalk Elvis cringed anyway.

He felt blood in his eyes. He could smell it and taste it, and he wondered how he could possibly know what blood smelled or tasted like.

He crawled to his feet as the siren moved closer. He squinted and saw the flashing blues of Formosa Beach's finest and, in his peripheral eye, bathed in that blue strobe light, a shadow outline of a person standing to the side. Boardwalk thought it might be the guy who had been beaten up first, but he wasn't sure and honestly didn't care.

"Fella," the bystander said. "Are you all right?"

The police car skidded to a stop.

"Well, well, well," said the squat policeman, getting out of his car. "Somebody beat up the Boardwalk Elvis."

"They kicked the shit out of him," the bystander said.

"What happened?" the cop asked.

"I'm not sure," Boardwalk said. He put a hand on his head and felt the thin wisps of his own emerging baldness instead of Elvis Presley's pompadour. Baldness and blood.

"They kicked the shit out of him," the bystander repeated.

"I was walking home, and I saw somebody beating somebody up," Boardwalk said, leaving out the part about public urination. "I was just walking home, and I saw these guys . . . "

He looked down at his chest. His jumpsuit was spattered almost black in the darkness.

"You got beat up watching somebody else get beat up?" the cop asked.

"I was walking home and I saw these guys . . . "

"They kicked the shit out of him."

"No they didn't," Boardwalk protested, though the guy pretty much had it right.

"So are you okay?" asked the cop. Boardwalk had seen this particular officer before and knew that he didn't care for men who dressed up like Elvis. "Need to go to the hospital?"

"I just want to go home," Boardwalk said. "I just need to be home. I live two or three blocks."

"You don't need stitches?"

"No, I just want to go home. Want to walk home."

"I'll need to give you a ride," the cop said.

Boardwalk E turned to him. "What?"

The cop had his arms crossed with authority.

"I have to give you a ride home," the cop said, "so you won't sue the department later for not giving you a ride home."

"That's okay," Boardwalk said. "Really, I won't sue. I just want to walk home."

The cop stepped forward and put a hand on Boardwalk's arm.

"I'm afraid I insist," he said.

So Boardwalk got in and rode the three blocks. The patrol car pulled up to his apartment complex, lights flashing, and the cop gave the siren a little squeal when they stopped, just, he suspected, to attract some attention.

"Thanks," Boardwalk said, getting out of the car gingerly.

"Whatever," said the cop.

The patrol car pulled away with one last siren squeak, and Boardwalk saw a few of his neighbors out on their small porches, enjoying the evening. All were gawking at him, and he didn't blame them. Wig missing, blood all over. He tottered to the outside staircase and began limping up, passing an elderly neighbor he occasionally spoke with on such nights who was sitting out on his porch, having a cold beer. The old man looked in disbelief at the sight walking by.

"Simon," the old man said, "what in the hell are you doing?"

Boardwalk ignored him, focused on the stairs, moving a foot in front of the other. He lumbered up to his door and opened it. Marsha was there, and immediately she rushed to him and ran her palms on his bruising face, and put her arms around him, wailing like a widow. She supported his weight with her own and led him to the couch where he finally collapsed, and he looked up at his wife, smiled a broken, blood-bubbled smile, and said I'm home, baby. Home to stay.

SURVEY OF MY EXES

S
amantha W, 4th grade

Do you know I never meant to cause you pain?

> You did push me down on the playground once! I think you
> were trying to impress another girl. My mom still has some
> pictures of us when we went to that Valentine's dance at church.
> I can send them to you. We should keep in touch! We were a
> cute couple.

Do you forgive me?

> For pushing me down?

*Do you know that I still think of you fondly? That I appreciate everything
you did for me?*

> Oh that's sweet. I still see your dad around town sometimes. We
> used to worship together but now we're going Methodist.

Did you know that I was diagnosed manic depressive in my thirties?

No, no I didn't know that.

Did you know when I was unfaithful?

I know you kissed another girl (not the girl you pushed me down for) but I forgive you. I think I kissed somebody else just to get even with you. Oh, Tommy Harris. Do you remember him? He got killed in a car crash a few years ago. It's scary to think we're at the age where we can die.

Do you know that I'm finally better?

I didn't even know you were sick. But I'm so glad you're better! Are you on medications? I spent some time working with mentally sick people at the hospital. It was sad. I didn't stay there too long. I'm working with kids now. They're special needs and really test my faith!

Did you know that I loved you?

You kept pulling my hair, so I knew you liked me.

Susan F, 7th grade

Do you know I never meant to cause you pain?

Junior High is supposed to be painful, but you didn't cause me too much. Drama, sure, but no pain.

Do you forgive me?

Sure. Do you forgive me?

Do you know that I still think of you fondly? That I appreciate everything you did for me?

That's real nice. I thought about you for whatever reason right after my first was born. I'd actually forgotten about that. I was exhausted and delirious, and for whatever reason I thought about you. I was on pretty heavy drugs. Maybe that's why. Anyway, it was a good memory of you. I don't think about the other kind.

Did you know that I was diagnosed manic depressive in my thirties?

Kristy told me. I never saw it, but I hope you're doing okay.

Did you know when I was unfaithful?

Yes, I read about it on the bathroom wall. I remember eavesdropping on a conversation with you on three-way calling, when Jackie was trying to get you to fess up to cheating, and then you started hitting on her, too. But that's okay. That was a long time ago.

Do you know that I'm finally better?

You have a good sense of humor, so how bad can you be?

Did you know that I loved you?

Are you coming this way for Christmas? It'd be good to see you.

Anyway, I do know you'd be there if I ever needed you, if it ever came to that. The same goes for me, too. You know that, right?

Kathleen K, 10th-11th grades

Do you know I never meant to cause you pain?

I think you've got the wrong person.

Do you forgive me?

I think you're looking for somebody else. This is embarrassing.

Do you know that I still think of you fondly? That I appreciate everything you did for me?

You sound sweet. I hope you find whatever it is you're looking for.

Did you know that I was diagnosed manic depressive in my thirties?

Oh no!

Did you know when I was unfaithful?

How many times were you unfaithful to this girl? You should be more careful with people's hearts. There's little forgiveness for something like that.

Do you know that I'm finally better?

Again, wrong person here. But I'm still glad for you, I guess.

Did you know that I loved you?

If you really loved me, I'd know who you were.

Kellie B, undergraduate, sophomore year

Do you know I never meant to cause you pain?

Never meant to, never meant to. I suppose that makes it all better.
All about the intention, right?

Do you forgive me?

I don't even know where to start. I was nuts about you. For a while,
anyway. And then you got weird. Just plain weird. Jesus Christ,
you were trouble. I hope you got some professional help.

*Do you know that I still think of you fondly? That I appreciate everything
you did for me?*

Be more specific about this, please. It's been, like, fifteen years, so
how many times have you thought about me in that span, would
you say? Give me a number. Because I bet it's very low. I bet
it's five.

Did you know that I was diagnosed manic depressive in my thirties?

Did you know that I had cervical cancer? Please answer in twenty-
five words or less. Or how about the home invasion? Know about
that? I got assaulted in my living room while Bobby was gone, and
nobody in the neighborhood even called the cops. Five surgeries

in three years on my jaw and shoulder, over a flat-screen fucking TV. Do you even care? Forgive me if I'm not weepy about your little diagnosis. It's not that I'm unsympathetic, I'm not heartless, but . . . what's this for, anyway?

Did you know when I was unfaithful?

Nope. No fucking idea. Thanks for sharing.

Do you know that I'm finally better?

If Bobby knew you sent me all these questions, he'd find you and kick your sorry fucking ass.

Did you know that I loved you?

How dare you ask me that? Okay. I'm sending this back just so your hands shake while reading it. Because mine shook the second I opened up and read this fucked-up thing. I'm showing this to Bobby. You've got some balls, buddy. How'd you even get my address? Fuck you, Jody. FUCK!! YOU!!

Meredith G, undergraduate, junior-senior year

Do you know I never meant to cause you pain?

It's nice to hear from you. I've moved on since then . . . water under the bridge. I got married a while back, and we have a son. We're living in Anderson of all places.

Do you forgive me?

Yes, of course. Though it took me some time. I wasn't in a good place back then either. I'm sorry for that time I hit you so hard. I had no idea you'd bleed like that.

Do you know that I still think of you fondly? That I appreciate everything you did for me?

[left blank]

Did you know that I was diagnosed manic depressive in my thirties?

That explains some things and not others. Bipolar didn't buy all those drinks or make those late-night phone calls. Bipolar didn't say that thing about my mother. Bipolar didn't drive three hours to sleep with what's-her-name. I don't want to get into all that again.

Did you know when I was unfaithful?

Every time.

Do you know that I'm finally better?

This was maybe five years ago. I was in the kitchen working on dinner and all of a sudden this overwhelming cigarette smell flooded the whole room. I'd quit by then, and my husband didn't smoke, and I know this sounds silly, but it was such an overwhelming smell, right up on me, that I just knew you were dead. You were the first thing that popped into my mind. And I fell down on the floor and almost stopped breathing, I was sobbing so hard, until Sam came in and calmed me down. The whole thing was strange, like a panic attack. And I'm not an irrational person, no matter what you remember about me, and it was probably just somebody walking by outside and smoking, but it was like I wasn't in control. I was wrecked for days after that. I started to look you up and make sure you were okay, but I didn't.

Did you know that I loved you?

I still have some things of yours, I think.

Tabitha S, grad school

Do you know I never meant to cause you pain?

Uh oh.

Do you forgive me?

How many people have you sent this to?

Do you know that I still think of you fondly? That I appreciate everything you did for me?

You're not going to publish this, are you? Are you going to publish this?

Did you know that I was diagnosed manic depressive in my thirties?

Okay, you're scaring me. What's going on?

Did you know when I was unfaithful?

Oh my God, you are not going to publish this. Tell me you won't. Change my name at least. Give me a call and let's talk about it.

Do you know that I'm finally better?

I thought so, until I got this.

Did you know that I loved you?

All right. Let me preface this by pointing out that you asked, but if you really want to know, you know how many people told me I was nuts? Even your mom pulled me aside one time. Everything was worth it, in my opinion, even the bad stuff, except for the really bad stuff, I mean the epic bad stuff, and we might've worked through that but we just couldn't talk. You were a ghost back then. The only way I knew what you were thinking was to read what you were writing about, and do you know how lonely that was? How unfair? I never told you, but I knew exactly what that Martian Body-Snatcher/Space Prostitute story was all about. I could see right through it. Please don't publish this. How is it that you can tell the world these stupid personal things and not be able to look someone you love in the eye? I am in NO WAY consenting to your publishing this.

Shelley P, concurrent with Tabitha S

Do you know I never meant to cause you pain?

You brought me pain and I liked it, wink.

Do you forgive me?

I forgive you fine.

Do you know that I still think of you fondly? That I appreciate everything you did for me?

I still dream about you sometimes. When I get a certain kind of drunk, I think of you.

Did you know that I was diagnosed manic depressive in my thirties?

You knew what you were doing.

Did you know when I was unfaithful?

Well yeah. When you were unfaithful, I was there.

Do you know that I'm finally better?

I heard you'd settled down. That's probably a good thing. I was actually worried for you. You were balls to the wall, my friend. I still tell a few stories about you. People think I made you up.

Did you know that I loved you?

You kept pulling my hair so I knew you liked me.

No Name Specified

Do you know I never meant to cause you pain?

> But you never avoided causing us pain either. Isn't that right? Do you remember us?

Do you forgive me?

> We should be asking the questions. We should be surveying you.

Do you know that I still think of you fondly? That I appreciate everything you did for me?

> You never thought of us. Not while sitting beside us, opening doors, not while climbing on top, slipping underneath, sneaking behind. Neither pulling us close nor running away. Even now, these questions are not about us. You're curious who will respond, what will be said. Will you use this in your work? Will you think of us fondly in your story? Will we even be able to recognize ourselves?

Did you know that I was diagnosed manic depressive in my thirties?

> You cast no reflection in mirrors. You weave shadows and strike plagues.

Did you know when I was unfaithful?

> When we were our most faithful.

Do you know that I'm finally better?

One time you came to us with a weight we asked to carry ourselves. How strange to see you get off your chest what you could never get off your back. Did it never occur to you how we are like your life's work? We too are heartbroken, pretending to be beautiful. We tell lies in your favor.

Did you know that I loved you?

Tell us again. Tell us now. Take your time and say it right. Say it so our arms raise chillbumps as if brushed by a ghost. Say it so everyone hears.

GUILT CITY

Y ou build a city in your backyard and invite everyone you've ever wronged to live there rent-free. The place fills up quickly. People you hardly remember show up with their family and pets and a U-haul of their stuff, but you turn no one away. There's plenty of room, you say. You've built a high-rise apartment complex in one part of the yard, and the units are very cozy, if you say so yourself. There's access to laundry on the premises (in your basement) and a gym (your unused treadmill). There's a corner grocery store near the pear tree by the property line, just a few feet's convenient walk from the complex. (You wronged a grocer once; he works in the store and employs an old-fashioned charm.) Next to the store, a one-screen movie theater. On top of the theater, a bookstore with a coffee shop (you've wronged booksellers and baristas, *scads* of them). That's a very livable city, all in all. You take a look around and dust off your hands, happy with the result.

You think this is appropriate; you've always been the kind to remember your debts rather than your gains. And if your first thought was of yourself when your doctor showed you what he did, pointing with a pencil tip along the film—you looked at the darkened, calamari-shaped mass and said, That's *in me?*—your next thought was of all the people you'd wronged, and how you could make amends with them in the so-short time you had left. That day you began laying the cornerstones of what would become the apartment building and sent out the first invitations. It would've been nice if a few people had RSVP'd graciously, saying, That's really not necessary; that transgression is long forgotten, over and done with. But they began showing up and just kept coming. It seems you've made the mistake of trying to make things right in a down economy. Free rent is hard to pass up.

It's an emotional time when new people arrive, all of them so much older than you remember. Lines down their faces in the tracks of tears. You can't help but recall those younger, smoother, more trusting faces (frankly, those tighter and more attractive faces) that you once betrayed in big or small ways. Forgive me, you say. You cling to them and weep into their shirts. Everyone lets you cry it out. They rub your back tenderly, kiss the top of your head. There there, they say. There, there.

Then you show them to their apartment.

The new arrivals are greatly impressed by the city, and by the fact that you've built it all yourself, by hand. I never knew you had so much hidden talent! they say. You should've been a city planner!

Well you know, you say. I've been building this city for years.

Nevertheless, you've forgotten certain important things: a fire department, a police force, a medical center, a house of worship, a bowling alley, a bar. You field complaints for all these services and rank the requests according to 1) how badly you'd wronged the person making it and 2) how guilty you'd feel denying the request. Some of the original offenses were pretty minor, after all, and you don't want to be taken advantage of here. For each request denied, you give a full-page typed rationale as to why and a handwritten apology on the bottom. Finally the citizens of your town get wise and have your mother come ask you for whatever it is they want. Now on Sundays those so inclined can worship in the little chapel you've just built near the septic line where the grass grows neon. Your mother sits on the front pew of the sanctuary and wails into her handkerchief. Your father delivers the sermon. You sit on the back pew, feeling more than conspicuous.

You charge no taxes to live here, though there are constant requests for improvements as the city grows. Your mother comes to you with a stack of small square papers; she's put up a suggestion box in Town Square to help manage the flood of requests she's been getting. High speed rail, she reads off. Trash pick up twice a week would be nice. There's a big pothole at the corner of Elm and the septic line. She reads these off, half-dozen at a time. These good people are counting on you, she says. Why must you disappoint them? Why don't you give them what they want?

The next day you have a road crew out to work on the pothole, and the citizens complain about the traffic backup it causes.

It's true that you'd expected a full city, but never this bustling thing. Every day someone else shows up at your door saying, Remember me?

Remember how you wronged me? And once you're prodded a bit, you finally remember and have to let them in. The city you live in (not the city you built) sends two police officers to your front door to ask what the hell you think you're doing. I don't know what you mean, you say, trying to play it off. We've had some complaints that you're operating an illegal city in your backyard. That's absurd, you tell them. Nothing could be further from the truth. Meanwhile the apartment building towers over your house. A metro bus squeaks to a stop in your side yard, and people file out. The police officers stare.

You know exactly who called the cops on you. It's your next-door neighbor Jack. He's just the kind of old buzzard who knows where his property line is to the exact millimeter and would raise hell if you put a clothesline pole just beyond it. And it's true: the cornerstone of the apartment building is likely on his property, by about an inch or so. But let's see *him* fit all this in his backyard. That afternoon you see him out in his yard, watering his tomato plants, and you walk over to confront him. You called the cops on me! you say. He looks down and says, Ah, ah. You do that again, old man, you say, you call the cops on me one more time, I will come over here and mess you up. You hear me?

Then, about an hour later, you start to feel very guilty. You walk over and knock on his door and apologize profusely—all the stress of managing this city, you explain. You tell him about your illness, how you're trying to make amends. He accepts your apology and says, That's a very nice goal. He doesn't seem like such a bad guy, after all … just bitter, ill-tempered, and snippy as a terrapin poked repeatedly with a stick. You shake hands and thank him for understanding. He says Fine, fine.

Then he moves into one of the apartments.

With Jack out of the way, you claim his backyard for the town's expansion and build a public swimming pool. Hopefully your mother will get off your back now. You've made me so happy, she says, her wrinkled palm patting your cheek. Later that afternoon she's got her floaties on, enjoying the shallow end.

You try not to get too overwhelmed with all this work, try to keep focused on the important things—on the spirit of what you've done. This is about letting go, you think. About making amends. You should feel a sense of relief. After all, who knows how much time you have left?

In fact you've already said your goodbyes; there was a dance held in your honor at the city's new VFW hall, and everyone came out to pay their respects, everyone took a dance with you. Former lovers held you close one last time only to be interrupted by other former lovers cutting in politely, like in the movies. Old bosses took your hand and twirled you around a minimum number of times before they'd served their obligation and then went back to eating cake in the corner. The last two to dance with you were your parents. Your mother danced first, but instead of looking at you she looked at everyone else who was looking back at the two of you saying Awww. She threw her head back and kicked her legs up, enjoying the attention. I feel so young! she said. Your father danced with you last and said, Your mother is driving me insane.

At the end of the dance, as everyone began walking to their cars, or waited for the public transportation back to the apartment complex, you felt so filled with joy and love. It felt remarkable, living like this. No longer hiding from your shame, but putting your shame out back of your yard, in nice apartments. Goodbye, everyone! you said, waving. I leave this world with a clean conscience, and with so much love in my heart! I will be gone any day now, and I thank you for this sendoff! Goodbye!

A month later, still not dead.

The turning of a season and autumn approaching, the weather cooling. High school football in full swing. The team mascot is named after you, though the team is scrawny and uncoordinated and has a lousy record. At a Friday night game, some drunken fool sees you and calls out, Hey, you screwed over enough people to populate a *fuckin football team!*

You think, Never mind a whole city, jackass.

The first baby comes in late September, belonging to a girl you hit in the head with a kickball back in elementary school, Janice Somebody-or-other. The first death, which you always figured would be you, comes at the beginning of October, your old Sunday School teacher Mr. Bob Monk. At a church social when you were a kid, you were running around with a group of friends playing tag and knocked Mr. Monk down to the ground. He was a hundred years old even then, so it's a wonder he didn't disappear in a cloud of chalk. But no; he lived 32 more years, only to die in one of the apartments you built.

Monk's daughter and her husband come to claim the body, and she screams at you, Why was he even here? He was very ill. We'd set him up in a nursing home with round-the-clock medical care. You killed him, she says. Then they claim the body, and the city performs a touching service right in your town cemetery, the first gravestone. Buried forever in your backyard. No getting away from him now.

You killed him! his daughter yells at you graveside, and her husband has to step in and pull her away.

Then, after the service, Monk's daughter, her husband, and their traumatized young son move into an apartment. Counting Janice Somebody-or-other's newborn, that's one person out but four people in. Number of people now living in your city: 1,126.

Your city, you realize, will soon collapse into civil unrest, it's gotten so big. You think of experiments you've vaguely heard about with a bunch of rats in a tight space. Of course your bank account is threatening collapse, too. You've not collected a dime in rent or taxes, financing the city with five no-limit credit cards that you never expected to be alive to pay back. But here you are, now October, with a mild cough but otherwise not dead. The last statement you opened, the minimum payment was criminal, the principal balance a number you have never seen in print. You feel like calling the doctor back and saying, Why am I not dead yet, you fucker? But you still owe the doctor a small bill, and you'd be embarrassed to call back before you paid it off.

Meanwhile all the mail in your mailbox comes stamped with a red Final Notice.

You know exactly what this means: soon enough, power, heat, and water will be cut for everyone in the city.

You contemplate asking the people who live here for rent, though you just can't bring yourself to do it. You think of asking your mother and father for a loaner. In the end you choose to dodge the phone calls from collection agents, leave the mail unopened, and grind your teeth in your sleep. Your back two molars crack and break. The next teeth in line are worn down as smooth as creekbed stones.

November. The skies gray and chill. You spend Thanksgiving in your small house in front of the city with the shades drawn, telling your mother and father you're not feeling well enough to make it in, though that's a lie—physically you feel, unfortunately, fine. The calls from debtors stop for Thanksgiving Day but resume at 7 am on Black Friday. The utilities are still humming into December by some miracle, you don't know how, and you consider calling the utility companies and explaining your predicament, how the bills got so out of hand. In the end you decide to avoid the problem and do absolutely nothing.

You make it to December 15th.

You make it to the 20th, and every time you see a utility van on the street out front of your house, you have the feeling that it's slowing down and scoping you out, as if the utility company has put a bounty on you.

On Christmas Day the city still has power, heat, and water, and you're so relieved you feel like throwing up. You have Christmas dinner with your mother and father in their apartment, and when they ask what's been on your mind here lately, and you lie and say, I'm afraid of dying. Though you're flummoxed by how you're here. Then your mother gives you a big present in a red and green box, sparkly bow on top. Mother, you say. You didn't have to do this. (You feel terrible since you bought them nothing.) This might be our last Christmas together, your mother says, wiping away thin tears. Your father is in the kitchen, drinking milk.

You open the present. It's filled with square pieces of paper from the suggestion box.

When you look back over at her, your mother is shaking her weary head.

Why must you disappoint these nice people so? she says.

That night you have a dream in which you die and go to Heaven. St. Peter or whomever meets you at the Pearly Gates and leads you down streets of gold to a fluffy white cloud with a comfortable-looking recliner on it. You sit down, and he wheels in a TV/VCR combo with the name of your old elementary school stenciled on it. He says, Now we're going to review your life in full and talk about how you did, and go over the parts where maybe you made a mistake or two. When you hear this you say to St. Peter, You have got to be mother fucking kidding me.

You wake yourself from the dream with a start to an apartment of vacuum-sealed silence. Subterranean darkness. Freezing cold, breath in smoke. You're shivering so hard you feel like you're going to crack another tooth. For a second you think, This is it, I'm dead and I've begun my death rattle. Then you realize you're not dead: The power and heat are gone. Everyone in the city is now freezing and in darkness because of you.

You panic, half-in-sleep, and consider what you can even do at this point. Get in your car and drive until you run out of gas (which won't be far). Hide. You could kill yourself, and the shame almost warrants such drastic action. But in the end you sit in bed and shiver as you hear the city begin stirring in the backyard. People are coming out of their apartments, asking what's going on. You know what's coming next: soon they'll be knocking on your door. It'll be pitchforks and torches. It'll be your head on a stake. You listen to the quality of the conversation outside growing more agitated. When your doorbell rings, you crouch down deeper under your covers and ignore it, which only makes the agitation out back in the city grow. You think, I've got to do something, I've got to do something. But you are, as usual, completely paralyzed by your doubts, your fears, your powerlessness.

You should probably be used to this by now.

Finally you hear some strange noise coming from outside: not a mob rushing your back door, but the movement of heavy machines. Big diesel engines that whoosh exhaust and rumble your walls. You hear men shouting to each other whoa-whoa-whoa!

Then your doorbell rings again. It's the front doorbell this time, accompanied by a brash knocking that could only be policemen or some government official. There's a quality to the knock that is a sure command.

You open the door and see the two policemen from before, though this time they've brought warrants and clipboards and an entire demolition crew. The policemen say, Well well. Then they tell you they've received complaints from your tenants about the poor conditions, i.e. the power is out, and reveal that they have a court order to move this city right out of the neighborhood.

Move? you say. Not demolish?

It says here M-O-V-E, says the gruffer policeman, flicking the paper with his finger.

It seems this is the case—the construction men in hardhats and orange vests are dragging huge chains and affixing them to the corners of your property, your entire house and backyard. Huge metal plates are drilled into the earth and the chains are attached. Each link of the chain is as big as a cannonball. The construction men work as quickly as their union mandates.

You mean you're going to tow us away? Everything?

The whole damn thing, the policeman says. The construction crew starts dragging the ends of the thick chains together at the front of your yard, presumably to attach to some other, larger machine for towing. You step out in your bathrobe and look back at the city towering over your home. Such a noble goal, and you went in with the best of intentions, but now it's over. The chains running from all four corners of your property, the ends of them now being hooked together all at a point.

You walk out to get a better look.

What kind of machine are you going to hook this up to? you ask. What's even capable of moving all this in one piece?

Come here and we'll show you, the foreman says.

Then they connect the chains to a thick harness like two great hooks and dig these hooks into your shoulders. They've run a massive extension cord from the city with an adaptor on the end round as a hockey puck, dangerous prongs sticking out of it. Hold your breath! one of the construction men says, and he shoves the thing directly into your back with one great stabbing motion. You feel faint as the power in the city comes roaring back on.

Yay! everyone in your backyard cheers.

The buildings and streetlamps begin humming again. People start heading back into their apartments. Your head is swimming.

Now PULL! the foreman yells at you.

So you take a step, with great difficulty. It strains your back, pulls your spine tight. There is no way you'll be able to move this city, you know that, but after that first groaning step, which takes quite a while, the second one seems easier, if only slightly, and quicker to put your foot back on the ground; the third is easier still. It's uncomfortable, sure, but it can be done. You can carry this city around with you for the rest of your life, however long that turns out to be.

Where will you go? You have no idea.

How long until this snaps you in half? Who can say.

That's not your concern now, anyway. All your energy has to go toward moving one foot in front of the other. Telling your legs to work to move this huge weight. At least you've solved the immediate problem of the utilities, and everyone in the city is happy again. All of them being warmed by you now in a most direct way, all connected to you, living off your energy, and you've allowed them to do so. You think this is appropriate. Everyone will like you for it. And besides, just to look on the bright side for once—and perhaps, you think, you ought to do that more often?—there is something strangely comforting in this new arrangement, isn't there? Wherever you go from this moment forward, and wherever you end up, at least you know that you'll always be home.

YANKEES BURN ATLANTA

'd been named starting pitcher at the Braves Baseball Fantasy Camp, the Prime-of-Life League, and I felt the start an honor, my moment to be both excellent and man-like, the very reasons I'd come to camp in the first place.

I suppose there were a few more reasons that I'd flown down to Florida to play baseball with a bunch of strangers for a week, such as the trouble I'd been having at Independent Vikings of America, the insurance company where I work, which led to some occupational malaise, due to the fact that I hadn't sold a policy in months. Such as the quiet that followed my son's leaving home for the University of North Carolina, what the WebMD refers to as "empty nest syndrome." Such as my low self-esteem and high self-disregard, my receding hairline and widening waistline, my nearsightedness, my halitosis and hypertension, and my lack of rigidity in the act of physical love. But Fantasy Camp was my chance to make a fresh start, to rid myself of the mediocrity I'd become exceptional at. It's the great old story of middle-aged men triumphing over adversity.

Though at first it looked like camp might turn out to be one more gross miscalculation in my life. It wasn't exactly what had been advertised in the brochure. For instance, Fantasy Week was supposed to take place at Disney's Wide World of Sports Stadium in beautiful Lake Buena Vista. But there was a money dispute between AOL Time/Warner—they're the sorry bastards who own the Braves—and the Disney Corporation. So instead camp was held at some AA stadium in the middle of nowhere. I don't know where we were, really. It looked like the kind of place a mobster dumps a body.

Here's another for instance: in the brochure it said I'd get to rub elbows with former Braves greats, with Braves of Yesteryear. But that wasn't really the case. I got to meet Phil Niekro on the first day of camp, but he showed up not in a uniform but in a polyester suit like I'd donated to Goodwill twenty years ago, and instead of a ball he cradled a martini. He made a few introductory remarks about baseball, its romance, the import of the game on our national identity, et cetera, but then he got off track and started talking about this lady who lived next door to him who he was taking to court because she was growing shit-ugly trees in her front yard, and the gated community had eyesore policies, and he was Phil Fucking Niekro. He went on like that for a good twenty minutes, then lit a cigar and disappeared. That's hardly rubbing elbows. Instead we hung out all week with a gruff old goat named Sandy. He was shaped like a bowling pin and claimed to have taken a few at-bats with the

Braves in 1982, but nobody much remembered him. Sandy was more of a bourbon man.

"Listen up, candy asses," Sandy said, when Niekro went off to find his limousine. "I've been charged with turning you sacks of shit into ballplayers by the end of the week, and by God if I'm not steamed about it. *Look* at you. You know what kind of men have worn the Braves uniform? The same damn uniform you're going to squeeze your fat asses into? Real men. Brave men. Dedicated men. You got your Dale Murphy. You got your Hank Aaron. Phil over there. What about Babe Ruth, Rogers Hornsby, and Cy Young? Yep, yep, and yep, at a season apiece. And now *you* guys.

"I don't care what kind of high-rolling, jet-setting, candy-ass job you've got on the outside, for the next week you are *ballplayers*. That means you will eat, drink, and sleep baseball. That's right, you won't eat caviar and you'll put down the donut. You'll eat *baseball*. For the next week, you're representing the entire Atlanta Braves organization, and when you squeeze your fat asses into that uniform you'll be charged with keeping up a storied franchise that started in 1876, a long time ago."

Beneath the offensive, insulting, bastardly exterior, Skip was really a fine man. Skip is Sandy, I mean. He was the skipper of the team, not named Skip. Baseball lingo. At the meet-and-greet the first night, which turned out to be just us and him standing at the main concession stand with an ice chest of cold Miller Lite, Skip told us his obligatory tales of the diamond, his days in the minors and his literal span of days in the majors. He'd put on a shirt and tie for the party, even a sharp blazer, though he still had his baseball pants on, and he jostled his bourbon neat and smoked filterless cigarettes and told us how the game used to be. He said back then superstars and working grunts all smelled the same, "unperfumed." He said base hits were hard as building a house, and home runs had to be muscled out of the park. He said in those days the Braves team would roll in from a road trip and be back in the arms of the women they loved by ten, then back to their wives by midnight. It was a good one, though I'd heard the joke before.

That night the fantasy campers huddled into the concrete barracks where we'd be staying, like a bomb shelter aboveground—a block building with rows of rust-framed bunk beds, an open shower and busted toilet in the back, a pay phone for homesickness and a couple of corroded window fans that didn't do much besides make noise and breeze the cobwebs around—and we claimed our bunk beds and shook hands and acted uncomfortable. I could tell we were all in the same way: all of us in our fifties, uncertain about each other, uncertain most of all about ourselves, tentative to let our guards down or our trust up, afraid of the humiliation of failing in front of other men. You could see it in the way we carried ourselves—slightly hunched in at the shoulders, arms down at our sides—like trying to fold our bodies around ourselves for protection. All of us dressed in golf shirts we'd bought for the trip, or maybe that our wives bought, neatly ironed, tucked into khaki slacks which rode too high on us, the belts getting closer to our navels year after year. There was only one younger guy there, who looked about thirty, with his faded baseball cap and untucked tee shirt, and he shook our hands and said hello polite as the rest of us, though I wondered what the hell he thought he was doing here among so many manicured, insecure middle-aged men. I think we were all wondering that.

Just before lights out, when the men piled into the bathroom to brush their teeth and wash their necks and underarms, I went back to the pay phone and called home to my wife. I told her my hopes for self-actualization were high, despite the shitty conditions of the camp itself.

"I tell you, Helen, I really believe this is going to do it," I said. "The rut I've fallen into is about to break. Here is my chance to right the wrongs of my middle-aged life, to recover a sense of masculinity and self-worth that will guide me confidently into my twilight years. I'm *living the dream*."

"Drink your fluids," Helen offered. "Don't overdo it the first day. Just stretch and drink your fluids and have some fun with it. Everyone is there to have *fun*, Eugene. So just enjoy it."

Helen and I have been married thirty years. We've raised a son, endured sickness and health and all the difficult, heartbreaking monotonies of adult life, and she's always been the one to look out for me. It was her idea I come to Fantasy Camp. She saw the commercial on TV and TiVo'd it, made the right inquiries, and for Christmas gave me a glove with the brochure tucked inside. She told me to bring the glove to camp, and to use it to bring the cheese. Helen's interest in baseball is through marriage, but she knows the names of the players and their stats, knows the history and keeps track of the standings as much as I do. She also holds my hand when I cry. Sometimes I forget I'm a lucky man.

BY MID-AFTERNOON MONDAY, our first day of fielding practice, I thought I'd made a big mistake about recapturing hopes and dreams. We were terrible. We stunk the place up. We were the opposite of good. We let ground balls bounce right between our feet. We took pop flies square on the top of our heads. Our throws were high or wide or in the dirt, and a few actually found their way into the empty stands.

"What are you shitbags *doing*?" Skip yelled, popping up fly ball after fly ball for us to fudge. He yelled things like *plant your feet, squeeze the catch, eyes on the ball*, but after an hour he stopped coaching altogether and just started cursing, calling us horrible combinations of profanities we'd never heard before, the kind you know only if you've been in baseball forty-plus years. It was an honor, but still humiliating.

Our batting wasn't much better. We broke for a bag lunch around one—peanut butter and honey sandwiches, a child's pint of milk, a chocolate cookie for dessert—then stepped up to the plate for another few hours of taking the fun out of fundamentals. Skip lobbed the ball to the plate and watched the fouls fly, the zingers go straight back, the choppy grounders that were more mistake swings than anything, a few bloopers into the outfield he condescendingly referred to as "blasts." He said he'd seen better swings on ghetto playgrounds.

But after a while we began to loosen up, to show some signs of progress, despite Skip's anti-encouragement. By the time supper came around—the February sun setting early but in beautiful shades, clouds full of copper and rust—we'd worked out some of the nerves, took better cuts, made solid contact, or at least made better baseball *sounds*. I took a turn late in the practice and drilled one down the right field line, making the phantom first baseman in my head look stupid. Skip rewarded our moderate okayness by piling us into a rotten old GMC van with a muffler problem and driving us into town to Shoney's Big Boy for the all-day breakfast buffet. We crunched bacon and shoveled eggs and went back over our failures and successes of the day, made notes to ourselves, mental and otherwise, and discussed the direction our team was heading. Skip sat by himself in the smoking section, read a newspaper. When we caught him looking over at us he shook his head in mild disgust. But we knew it was just part of the act. Bad cop, bad cop. After all, he had bought us breakfast for dinner.

Back in the barracks the awkwardness of the first night disappeared and the feeling that replaced it was one of camaraderie, trust, the feeling of being a *team*. Grown men walked the barracks shirtless, let their flabby guts go loose and unselfconscious. A few walked around with bats over their shoulders, as if they might be called up to the plate at any moment. There were smiles all around, and jokes, the slapping of backs. We were cautiously optimistic.

Skip came in just before lights out and told us shitbirds not to get too worked up, we had a big day tomorrow. Our first game was scheduled for four in the afternoon, an exhibition between us and the AA Berkley Barons, whose worthless facilities we'd overtaken. "And you're gonna need to get up a little early tomorrow, shitbirds," he said. "So we can get you guys sized up for uniforms."

Hearing this put a shiver up our concrete barrack spine. Just the thought of putting on that heavy, uncomfortable, beautiful polyester raised chillbumps on us, made us realize that this was it, there was no turning back. We were the Braves.

"Lights out at ten-thirty," Skip said. "That's fifteen minutes, Betty."

But we were riding too high to sleep, so we cut the lights at ten-thirty, just for show, then brought out our flashlights. We huddled in a circle on the barracks floor, the cold concrete, and discussed our practice that day, what we should have done differently. We discussed baseball in terms both practical and philosophical, what it meant to us, and fantasized about what we hoped would happen when we were on an actual field in play, playing against another team. Marvin, an ophthalmologist from Selma, hoped he had the chance to charge the plate hard on a bunt attempt, make the throw to first off balance, both feet in the air, and get the batter by a step. Reilly, a mortician's assistant from Macon, wanted to hobble from the dugout in the ninth, his knees busted from a season of injury and abuse, barely able to walk, and hit the improbable home run that put our team into some kind of imaginary postseason, then limp around the bases with his fist raised. Jimmy, the thirty-year-old with the faded baseball cap, a grade school teacher from Myrtle Beach, said he wanted to steal home and that he'd been practicing for months back home, starting from his garage and stealing a doghouse. We went around the room that way, half-hidden in the spooky shadows from our flashlights, and one by one revealed our dreams for the field of play, from the fundamentally fundamental to the heroically remote to my dumb bunkmate Morris, who claimed to be from "all parts," and who had no real plan for the week, so long as it involved "bringing it." I said I wanted a breaking ball that defied the laws of physics, one that started in the clouds and ended on the outside corner. But in truth I just didn't want to bounce the ball to the plate.

But then, as the hour grew later, and the flashlight shadows on our faces grew longer, the conversation became more serious and we opened up regarding the real reasons we'd come to camp, and revealed to one another in a manner befitting daytime talk, or in the unabashed male bonding only professional sports or the approximation thereof can offer, the failures and disappointments of our lives. Our mediocrities, our mortalities, our once-rebellious and -groovy manes of hair. We were from all walks of life—insurance salesmen, car salesmen, mortician, AMWAY—but we found we shared at least two things in common.

One, we had all woken up one day in our fifties and wondered if this—what we had or had not done, did or did not have—was all there was, and we'd been stricken thereafter with an inexplicable, irrepressible sadness which settled into our lives just when we should've been enjoying life the most. And two, we all held a genuine if misguided, desperate faith that what we'd lost along the way might somehow be reclaimed. That, of all things, a week at camp might somehow jump-start the stalled engines of our lives, might grease the gears, spark the plugs, change the tires.

And we all liked baseball, so I guess we had three things in common.

Our stories and our symptoms were the same: our bellies were rolling out, we had hair in our ears, we'd never understood our fathers—fearsome, frigid, authoritative men, the kind of old time, don't-make-em-anymore men's men who wore sleeves even in the summer, who never paid for an oil change in their lives, who worked the same textile lines for forty years until they finished with Bolivian maps of burnt skin up to their elbows, whose idea of both affection and correction involved hitting you flat on the crown of the head with their palms – and we feared our sons didn't understand us, and who could blame them? We didn't fully understand ourselves. We were in a moment of male crisis.

Except for Jimmy the grade school teacher, of course, who sat in the circle and listened to our tales of woe and nodded along as if he knew, as if he *could* know. So we asked him, *What are you doing here, anyway? You're young. What are you, thirty? Why aren't you out living it up?* We wanted him to hear our story and learn from it. We wanted better for him than we had for ourselves. It's a cautionary tale. But Jimmy looked at us plainly and said, "I understand how you feel. Really, I do. I feel the same way." He nodded when he said this, looked us in the eyes, as if we should believe him.

"You don't know shit," Reilly the mortician's assistant said, shaking his Ichabod Crane head. "What can you possibly know at thirty? You don't know anything."

Jimmy looked at us looking at him, stone-faced in the half darkness, an ultimatum right there on the floor. Suddenly he looked sadder and older than thirty. He reached up and took off his worn Braves cap, and underneath it he was as bald as ambition. We cringed in spite of ourselves, hunched up our shoulders and deformed our hands into claws, made impolite cringing noises just to drive home the point, all by reflex. Jimmy had a look on his face as if he'd seen the looks on our faces before. "At seventeen," he said, "it just fell out."

We were stunned. We didn't know what to do. So we did what we thought best: we took him into our circle, gave him a group hug, welcomed him as one of our own. The world had gotten to him early. He was a casualty. He was one of us.

It was almost midnight by then and we knew we should hit the bunks, rest up for the big game. So having dispensed of the serious business of the night, we broke out our stash of candy bars and passed them around. A few men brought out baseball cards and began making trades. And then, around twelve-thirty, nervous for the day ahead, we crawled into our bunks, pulled the covers up to our ears, and fantasized about the glories of the game ahead until we drifted off to sleep.

THE FOLLOWING AFTERNOON, the Berkley Barons massacred us but good.

You could make the argument that we'd practiced too hard the day before. We'd all woken up stiff as a morgue, lumbered out of our bunk beds, groaned into the showers. Bending to tie our shoes was an act of faith. You could say we were uncomfortable in those scratchy, awful damn uniforms. Or that we were distracted by the crowd—our game was open to the public, and the public who showed up, almost seven hundred of them, baseball lovers or simply the unemployed, were clearly there to root for the Barons. With good reason, I suppose.

They came out and knocked us around. They came out and made us pay for being old, and uniformed, and ridiculous.

Merle, a fat druggist from Alpharetta, was on the mound instead of me, thank God. They hit him something like twelve times: down the left field line, in the gap between first and second, bloopers in the outfield, three or four out of the park. I could only sit in the bullpen and watch until I couldn't watch any more. In the seventh I managed an inning of relief and was happy to retire the side one, two, three. For the most part.

The game was finished quick, despite all the offense. The freckled starting pitcher for the Barons, a menacing Richie Cunningham-type, had excellent command of the strike zone, and the defense behind him were graceful and quick as gazelles, if gazelles played baseball. The Prime-of-Life Braves had only three baserunners all afternoon, two accidental base hits and one hit batsman, Morris, who was beaned in the fourth on the flabby part of his back, just for kicks.

After the game Skip loaded us into the GMC and took us to Shoney's for burgers and ice cream.

"You guys got your asses handed to you," he said, sitting at the head of the table instead of in the smoking section, showing solidarity. "There's no denying it. But it happens all the time. It's just part of the game."

"They *destroyed* us," Horace the centerfielder said.

"It builds character," Skip said.

"They *humiliated* us," bald-thirty Jimmy said.

"It's always darkest before the dawn," Skip said.

"They were impolite about it," I said.

"It's a world for the young," Skip said, wisely.

But a Zen lesson in how much we sucked was not the reason we were here, and hamburgers and cokes, though fine, didn't make us feel better. Even sitting in Shoney's, we couldn't help but feel ashamed of ourselves. Families kept glancing over at us with pitying looks, like grown men out in public dressed as the Braves signaled we'd arrived on the short bus. Or maybe some of them had actually seen us play.

Skip gave us the night off and we spent it back in the barracks staring off into space. None of us called home to tell our wives about the game, though we'd all promised to, nor did we talk about the game with each other, even though we knew full well what it was we weren't saying. It was possible Reilly might go back to dressing corpses, little more than one himself. It was possible Merle might return to the pharmacy no more a watcher of the walking dying but a sad confederate. It didn't seem like exaggeration to us. We'd risked our pride in coming, and it seemed an imminent possibility that not only might we leave here every bit as lost as we were when we'd arrived, but we might've paid three thousand dollars for the honor. Fear is what men my age have instead of sense.

It seemed there might be an opportunity for self-actualization the next afternoon, Wednesday of our week, when we were finally scheduled to play our first major league game, an exhibition between us and the aforementioned, much-advertised Braves of Yesteryear. But the old men who showed up looked like they might've played for the Boston Braves. They barely made contact with the ball, swung defensively more than anything, and feebled toward first on fragile hips and fake knees. Sliding into base might've killed them. We beat the hell out of them 12-3. I pitched two innings of relief as fulfilling as kicking a dog.

I thought the whole thing was going be a wash after that. Back in the barracks the men wept out loud, called their families, described the sorry triumph. Skip came in later that night to congratulate us, took one look around the barracks, and said we were the sorriest sacks of shit he'd ever seen. Who gets upset when they win? Who cared that we'd beat up on old men? We'd beat up on *major league* old men. We might've gone out there today and beat up on somebody Joe DiMaggio once beat up on. It was something we could tell our grandkids.

This didn't lighten our moods.

That night we talked about making a break for it. To hell with self-actualization; the least we could do was salvage what dignity we had left and use it to catch a bus out of here. Horace, the centerfielder, suggested we sneak out in the middle of the night, follow the dirt road into the nearest town, use a pay phone to call our wives to come and get us, though why we couldn't use the phone five feet away was lost on me. Someone else suggested we go into the woods around the stadium and hide until camp was over. We could build a fort, live on lichen and wild berries. My bunkmate Morris suggested we strike, which got him sucker-punched a few times. But in the end, after the sniffles dried to crust, we decided we had only one choice. We were *ballplayers*, goddammit. We had to play ball, like it or not.

We all nodded our heads with appropriate masculine resolve and reverence for the game that this was so. Then, our begrudging course of action decided, we broke out our candy bars. Morris had a *Playboy* and passed it around, and we made jokes about the boobs, though we were secretly fascinated by them. And finally, after midnight, we shut off our flashlights, crawled into our bunks and replayed the horrors of the geezer game in our heads into our dull, dreamless sleeps.

But in baseball, as in life, each new day brings a chance for redemption, and when Skip came in the next morning, he brought us ours—we had the Yankees.

It was the Friday game, the big intramural between our Fantasy Camp and theirs, our chance to feel like real ballplayers. We'd even be taking a bus down to Tampa, and it promised to be a long, uncomfortable ride, just like the pros of fifty years ago.

"Now listen up," Skip said. He still had on his bathrobe and slippers, and there was powdered donut ash down his cheeks. He sipped from his coffee cup, *100% Bitch*. "I've had enough of this sacksacking around. So you played one game and you stunk. So you played another and beat the elderly. Well now it's time to pony up, boys. You've got one more shot for this Braves organization, one more shot to prove to me and to yourselves and to the world, at least the world who cares, that you are not merely weekend warriors, not simply sacks of fat tied off at the neck, that you are *ballplayers*. It's not going to be easy. You know who these bastards are. They're the goddamn *Yankees*. They handed it to us in '96 and again in '99. Do you *remember?*"

We remembered.

The Braves had struggled their way from worst to first in the miracle season of 1991 and had gone to the World Series that year and every year of the next few, save one, the year the Phillies had a team that looked like they could tell me what was wrong with my carburetor, and '94, when there was no series. Atlanta finally won it all in 1995, glorious triumph, but then the next year the Yankees showed up. In the first two games of the World Series the Braves beat them soundly, as a team of destiny should, and it looked as if the Braves were about to repeat as World Champions. It was going to be sweet.

Then things went to hell. Back in Atlanta the Yankees squeaked a game three win, 5-2. The Braves got back on track in Game Four, or so it seemed, scoring four in the second and tacking on some insurance in the third and the fifth. Six to nothing. It was a done deal. But the Yankees scored three in the sixth to close the gap, and in the eighth, Jim Leyritz, that dough-faced son of a bitch, stepped up with runners on against the Braves' closer Mark Wohlers, worked the count 2-2 by fouling off what they call sharp cheese, then belted a ball to South Carolina. Tie game. The Braves never recovered, blowing the game 8-6 in the tenth, and blowing Game Five the next night, a pitchers' duel between Andy Pettitte and John Smoltz, 1-0. Two nights later the Yankees clinched the World Championship back in New York, and it's not been a reasonable world since.

In '99 it was even worse. The Yankees were merciless. They stormed into the Series with their pretty boys and their million-dollar bills and their deodorant sponsorships and claimed the unofficial title "Team of the '90s" in a shameful four game sweep. *Yankees Burn Atlanta*, the dumb headlines read, I guess because *Yankees Sweep Atlanta* would've sounded like they were being helpful.

Thus ends the story of how the Yankees became our most hated and feared rivals.

Of course, other teams beat Atlanta in the World Series in the 90s too: the Twins and the Blue Jays. Do I hate those teams? Yes I do. But there are other factors at work here. It's Atlanta versus Yankees . . . *Yankees*. It's a grudge.

But all that past was prologue, Skip said between sips of coffee. Now it was our turn.

"I don't have to tell you, this is the reason you're here," he said. "It's going to be tougher than those Berkley Barons you pulled up your skirts for. But I know in my heart that we are *men*, Betty, and that we'll make a good show of it." Then, almost an afterthought, he looked over at me and said, "Barnes, you got the start."

This wasn't a revelation to anyone. I was the third pitcher of three, after all, and it was my turn to start, and furthermore his delivery wasn't exactly the moment in a movie where the music comes up. Nevertheless, hearing those words I was thrilled and terrified just the same. Soon as Skip left for more coffee, I called home and told my wife the news.

"I can't believe it, Helen," I said. "Here's my chance, finally, to do something extraordinary in my life. It's my chance on behalf of the entire Atlanta Braves organization to give them Yankees the what fer. I just hope I don't blow it."

I fully expected my wife to be supportive of me, to say the right thing, whatever that was . . . maybe something about the triumph of middle-aged men over adversity, or at least to tell me how much I wasn't going to blow it.

I didn't expect she'd go one further.

"Do you think I could come and watch you?" she asked. "I'd love to see you pitch, Eugene. And Bobby said he'd like to come, too. He has a buddy who'll drive. Of course, he doesn't know you'll be starting pitcher against the *Yankees*. I'm *sure* he'll come see you now."

Did I, at that moment, foresee the possibility of failure in front of my family? Yes I did. Did I foresee the possibility I might in fact *humiliate* myself in front of my wife and son, a man's ultimate nightmare and the subject of many made-for-TV movies? Yes. But I'd come to camp to claim importance for myself, to stake out my section of bravery, resilience, things like that. What good were those words now if I didn't walk the walk, toe the line, carry a big stick? It's like Yogi Berra once said, though I won't quote it here, because he was a Yankee. Besides, Helen was holding on, waiting for an answer, and I just didn't see a graceful way out of it. So I said, "Helen, I promise to make you proud." Strange how much easier it felt when I had only Braves history on my shoulders. But now I had to put the entire weight of my manhood on my back.

That night I learned many of the men felt the same . . . not about my manhood, of course, but about their own. We were all worried we'd blunder in front of our families. That we'd be the one to commit the error, misplay the ball, stumble on our own damn feet, whatever it was that would cost us the big game. But as we talked about our fears, we realized that at least we were united in our anxieties, and that none of us were enduring them alone. We were a team, goddammit. The last team I'd been a part of was at Independent Vikings of America, where they passed me up for a promotion and gave it to a college boy named Cameron who promptly called a meeting and said we were all part of something called the "quality team," and that "quality team" had no "I," even though *quality* does. But this was different. Here we were not united by that worst of motivations, a company's bottom line, but by our own bottom line, which was simple—we wanted to make our families proud.

It's a reasonable thing for men to want.

THE RICKETY BUS RIDE down the next morning—the bus shook like we were trying to break gravity—the men and I engaged in positive reinforcement, to take our minds off the fact that we were nervous as hell. We recounted tales from Braves history of men struggling against hardship and coming out on top. There was the 1914 Boston Braves, who rallied to win 68 of their last 87, going from fifteen out to ten up and finally to sweep the War-to-End-All-Wars World Series. And then there was the '91 team, a favorite example of washouts making good. There was the story of Sid Bream, who in the deciding game of the '92 NLCS scored from second on a seeing-eye single to advance the team to the Big Game, despite the fact that his knees were made of space-age plastic. And of course there was the fabled Hank Aaron, who broke Babe Ruth's all-time home run record and who was, as you know, black.

But as soon as we saw the stadium, the positive reinforcement ended and the nervous farts began.

Our bus passed through high, ornamented gates which had wrought iron baseball bats on top like the spires of a castle. We shook to a stop in front of the stadium itself, which gleamed like ivory. We had to avert our eyes, pull down our shades, even to look upon it.

Skip waddled off the bus, grabbed his gear from the underbelly, and told us candy-asses to move it. He led us in through the players' entrance, through the climate-perfect fairways of the stadium lined with men and women in tuxedoes standing behind wet bars, some holding silver trays with champagne and dangerous-looking hors d'oeuvres. I reached for one as I passed and had my hand smacked. He led us down the stairs to underground, or what seemed like the underground, through to the visitor's locker room, which looked like it had been ordered from some catalogue magnates pass around behind the middle class's back, and then through to the dugout.

Then we caught glimpse of the field. It was a brilliant, blinding, unearthly green. It was the color money would be if it breathed.

"Jesus," I said.

"You ain't kidding," Skip said.

The stands were already bustling with fans, and I strained from the dugout to see if I could spot my family. I glanced around at my teammates, who had this stunned, bloodless look on their faces. All that talk on the bus of famous Braves triumphing over whatnot apparently hadn't stuck. Sitting on the dugout bench, staring off at that pristine field, they looked like men waiting to face a firing squad. Fans continued to line their way into the seats. I could hear a few already starting up a chant. *Let's Go Yanks*. Or maybe it was *Scalp Those Braves*. Whichever, it was highly insensitive.

"Alright," Skip said, using his surly, I'm Motivated voice. "Let's go take BP."

The Braves Fantasy Team, Prime-of-Life League, didn't move.

"Come on, shitbags!" Skip shouted again. "Batting practice! Time to be men! Now grab a bat and leave this goddamn dugout!"

Begrudgingly the Prime-of-Life Braves stood and walked over to choose the rifle we'd be shot with. Skip clapped his hands together, then charged out onto the field; it was like *Braveheart* with Wilfred Brimley in the lead. As the team followed suit and gave up the safety of the dugout, the crowd began to boo. I didn't have to go, because of the DH, so I stayed behind and watched practice. Skip lobbed the ball toward them maybe five miles an hour, but the batters, scared shitless, swung through air, which sent the crowd roaring with catcalls and laughter. It was the saddest thing I'd ever seen. Every miss increased the odds that the next batter would miss too, until finally it looked like they were having trouble just holding the bat upright, like they were trying to swing a barbell.

Mercifully, BP finally ended—Morris looked like he was trying to bunt, the dummy—and the team scrambled back to the dugout while fans chucked foam cups full of beer down on them, having their fun. But Skip didn't let on if he was worried, and he warned us not to get our spirits down or our blood pressures up. He clapped his hands a few fast times and did the Let's Go. He pumped his fist and did the Yeah. He said maybe the batters should choke up more.

"You'd better go get loose," Skip said to me. He slapped me on the shoulder like buddies do. "You're throwing the heat today, boy." I knew in my heart that he knew in his heart that I had no heat, but I appreciated the gesture just the same. He pointed me to the bullpen, and I was grateful I didn't have to warm up in full view of the riot out there, like my teammates had, but as I started toward the pen the Yankees team ran out for their warm-ups and, big mistake, I hung out for a moment to get a look at them.

The Yankees men filled their uniforms like men. Muscular and fit, not a beer gut among them. I watched them take the plate and crush the ball, many of them knocking it right into the stands, and the throngs responded with as much enthusiasm to their swings as they had derision to ours. Shutters clicked. Grown men did the Arsenio dog woof. Women threw undergarments. Each batter dug in, choked up, and clobbered the ball into the ionosphere, one after the other, every batter up. If you closed your eyes it sounded, the hits and the noises of the crowd, like a thunderhead rumbling.

It took me a minute to realize just what I was seeing. I think I was paralyzed from the bladder up. But the next batter knocked his pitch into the stands with a round, feline, powerful swing. It was very recognizable. So I recognized it.

"Wait one fucking minute," I said, shaking my pointer finger at the field. "That's not the Yankees Fantasy Camp. That's the fucking *Yankees*."

It was true. Derek Jeter stood at the plate with that stance of his that looked like he's doing the plate a favor. He put another ball into the cheap seats.

My teammates clambered to the front of the dugout to see for themselves, and almost immediately the swearing began. It was *what the fuck* and *what the hell* and *what the shit* this and that. A few of my teammates, a bit goosey from the hardships of the week, broke down in tears.

Skip put up his hands defensively as if to ask What's the problem? "I *told* you you were playing the Yankees," he said. "Didn't I say that? Right?"

"You said Yankees," I shouted at him. "But you didn't say it was the *New York Fucking Yankees!*"

Skip spat out a sunflower seed that stuck to the side of his face.

"I said, Barnes, you're starting Friday against the Yankees. *Tell* me I didn't say that."

Yes, that's what he'd said, I said, but surely he could see how I might've misunderstood him.

Skip chewed on his sunflower seeds and adjusted the seam on his crotch, then began a long story, the point of which was, this was how Steinbrenner liked to spend his Februarys. He always brought the Yankees down to play against the fantasy-league teams so he could sit in his luxury box with his roast suckling pig and fresh pineapple slices and the finest champagne and a bottle of baby oil, and he feasted on pig until his skin glazed and sipped champagne until he was high, then he baby oiled himself and watched the Yankees beat the living hell out

of some pitiable fatass team like ours and quote "pleasured himself."
The Yankees Fantasy Campers themselves had been sent down to
Venezuela, where they sat for dark hours in a warehouse without proper
ventilation, stitching baseballs and finishing Yankee merchandise.

"This is no *secret*," he shrugged, like he thought we should've
known. "It happens every year."

The public address announcer welcomed everyone to this
exhibition between the Atlanta Braves Prime-of-Life Fantasy Camp
and Your New York Yankees.

"Shouldn't you go warm up?" Skip asked.

"I won't do it," I said. I dropped my glove. "I'm not going
out there."

"Yes, you goddamn will!" Skip fired back.

"No I won't."

"Yes, you will!"

"No I won't."

"Yes you will!"

"You can't make me," I said.

Skip lunged and grabbed me by the shoulders, and for a moment
I braced myself for a head butt. But instead, he stared me straight in
the eyes, said nothing, just stared and breathed through his nose. In
another context, out in the real world, such an embrace would be
embarrassing, or threatening. It looked like he might be getting ready
to kiss me. Or perhaps it was the head butt after all.

"You may be a rookie, Barnes" he said at last, whistling through
his nostrils, "but by God, you are a *Brave*. You are in the *dugout*. You

are in the *uniform*. You have a frikkin' *tomahawk* on your chest."

I dropped my head and saw that he was right. Out of the corner of my eye I saw the other men looking down at their chests, to see if they had one, too.

"They're going to kill me," I said, looking back up at Skip.

"They certainly are," Skip agreed.

The PA read off our lineup and the booing in the stands resumed.

"I can't throw for shit," I said. "My *family* is out there."

"Barnes," Skip said, "I have a story which I believe fits this occasion perfectly. It's about my father and my relationship with him. It's sentimental and momentous, and the payoff is my father looking at me and saying, Going Home. But I don't have time to tell it to you now, so just pretend I did. The point is, go out there and pitch like you've got a pair."

I realize now that with the noise of the crowd I couldn't possibly have heard what I thought I did at that moment. But I swear, standing there, staring my skipper in the face, my teammates looking to me for leadership, that I heard my wife's voice rise above the ridicule of the crowd, rise above the stadium itself, telling me I could do it. I swear I heard my son and his drunk frat buddies holler something about the triumph of middle-aged men over adversity, about the links between fathers and sons, et cetera, and yelling for those Yankees to come get some. I swear I thought my teammates began slow-clapping, like in the movies. Maybe I was having a mild stroke.

I retrieved my glove from the dugout floor, slid it on, smacked my fist a few hard times into the leather. "I'm going to need a ball," I said.

Skip reached into his pocket and pulled out a baseball. He handed it over and told me to give them hell, and he called me Stumpy. It was the first nickname I'd ever had.

I raced out of the dugout and back toward the bullpen, ignored the catcalls, dodged the beer cups, and had time to throw a dozen or so warm-up pitches before our leadoff batters struck out swinging. Then, my moment come, I charged out of the bullpen for the mound, ignored and dodged the et cetera, then took my place on the rubber. My rightful place. The rubber I'd waited all my life for.

I faced twenty-one batters and gave up twenty-one hits, all of them homers. I went zero-thirds of an inning.

But it didn't matter, because I didn't see any of it. See, my brain seized as soon as I let go of the first pitch, so I didn't watch the unloading that followed, didn't hear the howls of laughter from the goddamned Floridian Yankee fans. In my mind, the last thing I saw was that first fastball hanging in the air, halfway to the plate, and it had not yet been crushed, had not yet left the park. Maybe the reason I say this is because this is the only picture Helen took, the only picture I still have from my start. Or maybe she took fifty of them, I don't know, but Helen is a good woman, and she loves me, and so the first pitch is the only one that remains. I have it framed at my desk at Independent Vikings of America, and many of the men I work with come into my office just to look at it. In that picture it is still a perfect game, the ball forever untouched. In that picture there is possibility. Maybe the batter swings and misses. Maybe he's taking right down the middle. In that frozen moment I am balanced on one leg, my arm extended, and the small white ball is resting there, faultless, a strike all the way.

FUTURE ME

1

Future Me arrives in my office on a Tuesday afternoon and tells me he's me from the future. He looks exactly like I would look if I stopped smoking cigarettes and started smoking army boots. His complexion is terrible. He smells like bourbon. He is clearly not me from the future, just some homeless person who bears a strong resemblance to me and knows very intimate details of my life when I ask for proof. I'm not falling for any of this, I tell him. You'd better get the hell out of here. You're wild-eyed and crazy, you reek of liquor, and you're wearing what appears to be a Cosby sweater. You look like a man who's made a lifetime of very bad, even insane decisions. He raises his eyebrows and arms simultaneously as if to say, Yeah.

2

Three years later he's back. This time a Wednesday. I say, Wait, who are you again? Then I remember. Oh god, I say, it's *you*. I haven't seen you in three years. What the hell are you doing here? He says, For me it's been the blink of an eye. I went back to my time-travel ship after you kicked me out, and then came straight back here. For me it was almost instantaneous. So I say, Why in the hell did you go back to your time ship, if you knew it was going to spit you out three years later? Last time you were here, you said you were from the future, which made me think that whatever your mission was, it was, oh I don't know, urgent. So why even go back to your time machine at all? Answer me that. He says, Because I had to go to the bathroom. But there's a bathroom right down the hall from here, I say. Why go back to your time ship just to go to the bathroom? He says, Because it was number two, and I've never been able to go number two in a public restroom. I'd rather my bowels rupture than go number two in a public restroom, I get so embarrassed. I know it's strange to say, he says, but it's true. Then I say, Oh My God very dramatically, because now I'm convinced he's actually me from the future.

3

I say, Tell me what happens. Is there some future calamity? Is the world going to end? Are we invaded by Martians? He says, The world's fine, but you are a complete mess. You're the calamity. You've never been married. You have few close relationships. You stare out windows when it's raining like in a drug commercial. Your alcohol and pornography use, let's just be honest, they're off the charts. You smoke way too much. You're afraid of your own shadow. You live a sad, sad life. You've got to change, and I've got to change you. I mean I've got to change *me*, and there's no time like the past. I ask, How many novels have I published in the future? He says, Two. To very middling reviews. I say, What must I do?

4

He says, In the future you are a sad asshole. There's no other way to say this. You're already in a holding pattern with your life. You're sealing my fate right now. Right at this moment, with your fear and your inertia, you are dooming me. I say, No, no, these are my office hours, and he just looks at me.

5

Okay then, I say, because I think I've got him. So why are you coming to me now? If I'm already in trouble? If we're already doomed? Why didn't you come to me, like, in my twenties? Or, like, still in high school? As a kid, even? Why didn't you wake me up as a kid and tell me I would be visited by three ghosts or something? Why set your time machine to now, if the problem already exists?

6

Future Me says, Because I remember this time in our lives as being our best. When we were most in control, relatively healthy. Relatively sane. I think of you, I mean us, right now as maybe the most capable we ever were. I say, You're kidding me, right? I think you must have your wires crossed somewhere. (But actually, it's rather nice to hear.)

7

There are still a ton of questions I have about the whole thing, before I'm willing to commit to any kind of time leap—logical inconsistencies, for one, which seem especially an issue where time travel is concerned, if the literature on the subject is to be believed. Look, I say. If you can just grab a time machine and go back and change the past, then why isn't everybody doing it all the time? Everybody does, Future Me says. That's why it seems like life is such a mess, like there's no rhyme or reason, no cause and effect. Nothing in charge. The rules shifting beneath our feet. The center does not hold. That's what time travel does. That, my friend—he says—is what life does. And while none of this should probably make any sense to me—just a bit of sci-fi time-travel doublespeak—it actually explains quite a lot. All those terrible ideas that seemed so good at the time. All those goals I pursued that proved substantial as ash. All that love that went away like wisps of smoke. I've always suspected some terrible randomness in control of it all, just like that.

8

Okay, I say, I believe you. So where to now? I mean *when*? He says, I'm not sure. We need to plan this out. We want to make as few changes as possible, in as few times as possible. Otherwise, we might end up crisscrossing ourselves. Undoing what another group of us just did. We need a light touch. You mean, I ask him, that we've only got one chance to make this work? No, Future Me says, I mean we've got a million chances. I just don't want to fuck them all up.

Then I remember something I'd totally forgotten about—one night in my early twenties, two guys came up to me in a bar and told me they were Future Me's. I told them, Get the fuck out of town. I remember they were dressed strangely, one in futuristic garb and the other in a Cosby sweater. They looked like father-and-son leather goods somebody forgot to oil. These strange fellows told me, We're not going anywhere before we talk some goddamn sense into your goddamn head you stupid fucking asshole. I said, Well, well then. If we must talk about serious things, you odd fellows, let me at least buy us a round of drinks. They said No, no drinks, no way, but that only lasted about a minute before I was bringing three whiskeys and three purple hooter shooters back to our table right by the corner jukebox and had proposed a toast to these two crazy guys in my bar. I remember they said Cheers. The rest of the night was kind of a blur. I believe we shot pool. Cutthroat. I don't recall who won.

So I tell Future Me, I just remembered something. In my twenties. That's when we go back. But we won't be successful. I remember it now. You and I came up to me and you at a bar and tried to warn me, but I got you and me drunk instead. I think all three of us might've gotten lucky that night, with that girl who used to hang around. The one with the tattoo of the baboon on her boob. Remember her? Hell, I might even be my own father for all I know. That girl could be our mother, and all three of us could be our own fathers. Future Me says, God you are a fucking idiot.

11

But he heeds my advice nonetheless—Future Me has no memory of me and him coming to see him and me at the bar, though he does have a memory of me telling him that we did, from when I told him just now. So I cancel my office hours for the rest of the day and we walk across campus to his time machine. It looks like a giant egg. The kind of brown plastic egg pantyhose used to come in back in the '70s. It is, without a doubt, one of the least stylish vehicles I have ever seen. I don't know what I was expecting, but this isn't it. What the hell? I say. They don't have European hot rods in the future? No traveling in style? Future Me looks down at his feet. The egg is all I can afford, he says. I've been driving it for years.

12

Streams of pulsing light. My chest pulls away from my body. Ghost images float past: a round clock spinning backwards. Calendar pages. Stonehenge. Old girlfriends. The Mona Lisa. Sharp words. Errors in judgment. Pilgrims. Broken trusts. Abraham Lincoln. Unreturned phone calls. Missed opportunities. The ones that got away. The things I tried to hide. Old Top 40 radio. William Shatner. A brontosaurus chewing leaves with its old man mouth.

13

Past Me is in a bar. Hair down to his shoulders, devil-may-care attitude, slinking around like he owns the place. He has absolutely no plans of making it to class tomorrow. Flannel shirt and shit-kicker boots. I'd forgotten what it felt like, smoking in a bar. The air smells like beer and pizza and smoke, and Future Me and I are the only two people in the bar who look worried about anything. The jukebox holds actual CDs. A dead lead singer is singing, and he's still alive. Past Me hands out dark-looking shots to strangers, lights cigarettes, strikes pathetic poses. It's jarring and bittersweet and shameful. Future Me says, Focus.

14

It takes me a minute or two to work up the nerve. I light up a smoke right there in the bar—feels incredible—then I walk up to him and say, Okay, kid, now you listen to me, and I tell him that my friend and I are him, from the future. We need to make some changes, I say. It's time to put your life in order, study harder, be more responsible, get better with money. Of course he doesn't believe me. Why would he? I'm embarrassing even myself. If you're me, he says, name me five famous people, living or dead, that you'd sleep with, that no one else knows about, that you'd be terribly ashamed if it ever got out. And I say, You mean circa 1994?

15

I name them. Damn, he says.

16

We're here to talk some sense into you, I say. You're on a path that leads to nowhere. It's a sad path, and it leads to office hours at a small college in Ohio. This seems to concern him. And what do we do for a living? he asks. We're a writer, I tell him, we teach creative writing at the college level. Now he smiles and seems impressed. Relieved, in fact. In *Ohio*, I remind him. Never married, live alone. We rent instead of own. Always broke. Hardly enough time to write. Always depressed but we hide it well. We're lonely, but we can't do anything about it because we don't know how to connect with people. We're drifting out here alone, in a sea. He says, Writers are lonely people sometimes. I can see he's got all these romantic ideas in his head about suffering. I say, You should get used to that suffering, kid, because you've got lots and lots of it ahead. He shakes his head so that his long hair looks ruffled like Lord Byron's. I say, Oh sweet Jesus. You've got all the wrong ideas, kid, and you might regret some of them some day, when you get to be my age. I'll never live to be your age, he says sadly. I'm destined to die young. I say, Oh Jesus Christ.

17

Let me buy you a drink, Past Me says. You look old and worried, like you don't have any fun. I have fun, I tell him, lots of fun, but I don't press the matter. Come on, one drink? No, no, I'm on the clock, I pun. But the truth is I could use one. Especially back here, where my sense memory tells me to get drunk, numb the pain, and to put on a hard-to-watch show while doing it. Get drunk with me, Future Me—Past Me says—and let's think about things. Christ, you're not listening to me at all, I say, and I turn to tell Future Me that this kid is beyond help, but my Future Me's not there. He's on the other end of the bar, in a dark booth surrounded by kids in flannel shirts and long smelly hair and jewelry made out of hemp and they're all smoking clove cigarettes; even Future Me has one. There must be six or seven of them all packed into the booth, and Future Me is scrunched right up to a girl with a nose ring and low-cut shirt with her boobs spilling out, and sure enough, there's the tattoo, which I remembered being of a baboon but it appears to be a full-color Tree of Life from the ancient Kabbalah. Another kid comes back with a full tray of shots and passes them around. Future Me takes one, and I can tell he's wondering what kind of toast to make. He may or may not have told them already that he was from the future. What are you doing? I say. What the hell? These fine kids have bought me a shot, he says, raising his plastic cup. These are my new friends. We're not here to play around, I tell him. No shots. But he says, Just one shot couldn't hurt, could it?

18

We are the last to leave the bar at 2am, the crowd of kids stumbling and laughing and Future Me right in the middle. He's had one too many. Many too many. His frail arm is around the tattoo-girl's waist, he's got a nicotine-yellowed finger hooked into her belt loop. He can't possibly be serious. Come on, he says, these fine people want to go to the Huddle House for some grub, then we're going over to Gopher's. Gopher's got some marijuana he says he brought all the way from . . . it was from . . . hey, Gopher, where did you say that marijuana was from? What country was it again? Gopher? Hey Gopher. Gopher. Oh, I'm very sorry, Teddy. Where did you say it was from, Teddy?

19

This old fool. He doesn't understand he's being made fun of. This Cosby sweater. He believes he is twenty years old. His voice has become very loud. They're stumbling toward someone's car and he believes he is one of them. It takes two of us on the outside, me and Past Me, to see how sad this is, how hard to stomach. Past Me says, Okay. I get it.

20

This actually isn't quite the way I remember it. Already the details seem altered from the ones buried in my memory. You'll need to remember this moment *right*, I tell Past Me, so you can regret all of it later, in correct detail. The girl with the boob-tattoo overhears me and says, Or you could just accept your present moment without attachment or suffering, become greater than your rock. Camus, Past Me says, proud he got the reference.

21

It's four in the morning before we convince Future Me back to the egg, then he wants to drive. Past Me looks for the seatbelt but there isn't a seatbelt in an egg. Is there a coffee pot in this thing? I ask Future Me. You should really have some coffee. He says, I wanted to go hang out with Trisha. I think we really had a connection together. She did seem nice, Past Me says dreamily. (I admit, the Camus thing did it for me, too.) Okay, I say, now what? What year should we go back to? When did all this go so wrong? Then Future Me excuses himself, stumbles to the back of the egg where the bathroom is, and shortly begins to retch.

It is loud, violent, without the least concealment. It fills the entire egg with the sound. It lasts for a long while. Every time we think it's over, he ralphs again. Finally, he begins to whimper back there. That poor old guy is really suffering, Past Me says. I wish we could go back in time and convince him not to drink so fucking much. I say, that is a fine idea.

2 2

The controls in front of me look as simple as a clockface. I roll the hands back and grab the lever. You've got the right idea, I tell Past Me. Let's stop this drunk before it happens again. I pull the lever and there's a strange popping sound in my sinuses.

2 3

Past Me and I get out and go straight for the bar, intercept the first shot before Future Me has a chance to take it, and there, in a corner of the bar, we find Past Me, which is to say, another Past Me—it gives the first Past Me a great thrill to go up to the second one and say, I am you from the future, because they are twins, dressed the same way for a night out, and Past Me 2 is so impressed that he says without hesitation Fuckin A.

2 4

Then we're all back in the egg together: me, Past Me, and Past Me 2, and the Future Me who is still sober, and the Future Me who is in the back of the egg vomiting. I set the controls for 1983 to give that a try, and we're off. Streams of pulsing light. One-night stands. The pyramids. Nostalgia. Past Me 2 says, Hey, wait. How can we all be in this egg at the same time? Haven't we broken some fundamental law of physics or something? Future Me up front listens to the horrible sounds of Future Me in the back. His eyes are full of pity, hanging with tears. Nothing has changed, he says. I still can't do anything right.

25

Then, as we're hurtling through that cosmic lightshow, we pass ourselves in the time slipstream—another egg, I mean, which looks just like ours, right in front of us, like staring at ourselves in a mirror, and we can see through the windshield of the other egg that it's Future Me and me, and Past Me, and another Past Me, and then a wide-eyed Boy Me. Face and hands pressed up against the windshield of the other egg, mouth open, missing a front tooth, having the time of his life. The egg disappears suddenly and Past Me 1 says, Did you see that? We've breached the time continuum or something. That was us. I say, We've been back to the past already, in that other egg, as far back as our childhood. We must have breached the continuum when we went back to get Future Me. I told you, Past Me 2 says. Future Me, sitting at the controls, says, We may have needed to think this through a little more.

24

We pass another egg that contains us and them, then eggs that contain others . . . I spot one containing High School Me, desperate to get laid, another with Junior High Me in a terrible jean jacket I'd forgotten all about. That goddamn jean jacket. Zippers all over it in the knockoff-brand Thriller style. That goddamn jean jacket. Junior High Me's ego, I know, is too fragile to be seen in public in such a thing. He wanted a name brand and my parents bought a weird knockoff. Poor Junior High Me, with his look of terror and confusion. He wants so much just to be liked.

16

Flashes of light, the egg begins shaking. Light everywhere, the egg coming apart. Other eggs pass in front of us and their occupants look just as concerned. Future Me 2 says, Nothing has changed, I still can't do anything right.

11

Other eggs, they've followed the time stream back even further, to set things right. 1920s Me, which is some relative I do not recognize, but where the dominant gene must lead back to, his eyes sad like Buster Keaton's. Victorian Me, a poet in rags, and he's hanging on for his life. Medieval Me, Cro-Magnon Me, a damn heavy unibrow on him and suddenly I know where I get it from. How far back would you have to go to correct the mistakes of your life? Which was the first? Would you not have to correct every new one? Would you not correct this one right now? What do we do? Past Me 2 asks. I say, Keep going back! We've got to get ahead of those other jokers. Go backwards in time! Step on it!

9.1132

Backwards backwards backwards backwards backwards in time. But moving backward too fast. Much too fast. Speeding past history, into the formation of the Earth, and then past that, the cooling of plates returning to the molten masses and returning to cosmic fire, We're getting closer, I call out, and then to clarify I say, I mean closer to the moment it all went down! A second later I say, We're getting closer, and then to clarify I say, I mean closer to the moment it all went down! And I mean the universe, everything. Johnny Carson monologues and that backdrop blue curtain. Primordial ooze. Next-day phone calls. Backward, backward, backward. Archers on horseback. Albums on cassette. How easily I betray trust. Action figures sold separately. John Lennon shot. Old mistresses. T-Rex. Tears. More tears. More tears. Repeating on repeat, the faces of Me staring back from the other eggs in all this light borealis space breathing dropping eggs all of them me dropping down in front of us (what's laying these eggs?) how many times have we done this now the same mistakes over and over and over and

7.536274621763

I think it's my fault, I say to Future Me 2, for going back to get you. I think it's my fault, I say to Future Me, for going back to get you

5.74345788665439843457

I think it's my fault, I say to Future Me, for going back to get you the light ahead furious the universe retracting itself toward the light pulling us in and π

We've gone back too far! Up in front of us! It's the Big Bang! I say. It's pulling us in!

0

I think it's my fault, Future Me 2 says, for going back to get you

0

It's the Big Bang! I say the universe retracting itself toward the light Future Me says I can't do anything right

0

It's the Big Bang! the universe retracting itself pulling us in the eggs have merged and the Me's who were part of me staring dreamily into space caveman gawking at the trails these vibrations music is how it feels not in fear but awe but see his savage eye when he gets back he is taking the world in will remember it dreaming Cave Drawing Cave Drawing

0

We can't go forward, Future Me says. Only back. Something's fucked. With the controls. We're caught in the pull. We can't go forward Future Me says nothing has changed still can't do anything right Only back! Where it all began! iterations of myself decimal changed making the same mistakes the beginning of everything! someone says mistakes again someone says all of us the same space me and everyone all these other lives you will be nothing yet how far back would you go to correct the mistakes back to the beginning I think my fault he says for going back to get you

∞

pushed a tight ball feel myself smaller I do feel smiler strange sense of everything reasoned necessary all tears I think I have made versions of regrets tears equal to laughter in this place feel body dissolve

∞

component parts anti-parts don't exist in the light breaking apart we are made of tears become unfurled in the same space feel we were together there remember part of equal to laughter in this place back to get you apart of everything is needed in this breathing apart we are still there together remember and all of it necessary will be all feel so much pain and love and pain and love breaking apart of everything else and all feel

∞

all feel

∞

all feel

∞

...

∞

bang

BEARING A CROSS

Our town held elections in that year—not long after the terrorist attacks— in which Bible thumpers came out in support of a Bible thumper, elected him in a landslide, and voted to turn the town of Walhalla, SC, into a theocratic form of government. To our credit, I think we went into theocracy with the best of intentions. We were going to be a model for the rest of South Carolina and maybe the world. We would practice the Golden Rule, keep God's commandments, and most of all we'd be spiritually insulated from harm or terrorist attack.

Needless to say, the experiment ended poorly, with the town's churches marshaling their forces and small arms and then marching on Main Street. But hindsight's 20/20, as The Book says. Anyway, I don't mean that we intended to turn our town into the kind of crazy religion-state you see on National Geographic, with public executions, crushed dissent, military force, all that. We simply decided to give our town over to Jesus Christ and to enforce Old Testament law.

I mention the terror attacks because I believe they played an important role in our deciding to become Jesus Town. How could they not? On that terrible morning everyone watched what happened on TV—we either went home from work or never went to work in the first place. And those things we saw shook us: the plume of black smoke over the city, crawling around like some kind of beast, then people on the World Wide Web finding faces hidden in the smoke, devil-faces, horned and laughing. Then in the days that followed, to learn there was something called a jihad, a whole force of foreigners that followed Mohammed and who'd declared war on us, *all* of us. These things put the town of Walhalla on high alert. So South Carolina had about a zero chance of being hit, but that morning anything seemed possible. I called my sister down at the Piggly Wiggly and told her to go home for the day, she wasn't safe. At the Piggly Wiggly. That morning we were all New Yorkers—a kind of miracle in itself—and you could smell the sulfur burning off her buildings from here.

Of course our preachers did their part by preaching The End of the World at the Wednesday night service the next night. Really they'd been preaching it for a lot longer than that, but we paid attention now. A couple of local ministers claimed to've found reference to the attack in the Bible, to a tower being smote, but all of the sermons made it clear: Our days were numbered. Our children would never make it to their proms. We'd never see a Gamecock winning season. Out front churches changed the sign from The End Is Near to The End Is Here.

It's easy to see how we were letting our fears get the better of us, but what do you want? We lined up at the Food Mart for bottled water and canned goods and stopped at the hardware store for some duct tape and plastic. We went to the pawn shop and bought semi-automatic personal protection. And of course we hung our flags, dusted off our Lee Greenwood, located our Bibles, and we worried. I guess the only people in town who didn't rush right out for supplies were those who still had some left over, from the Y2K.

IN THE MIDDLE of all this apocalyptizing we voted for mayor.

For the twenty years before, our mayor had always been a guy named Buck, who'd managed to hold the office so long primarily because he always ran uncontested. In fact, because he ran uncontested you could hardly say he ran at all. He didn't print out any fliers or shake any hands. He was the only guy who ever wanted the job, so he got it. He spent most of his time sitting at the local lunch counter, drinking coffee with the other old men and smoking cigarettes. His pants bagged around his butt and every move he made was at half-speed. Once a year he'd get up on stage at Walhalla's main event, the state's only completely dry Octoberfest, and he'd sing half a verse of "Proud Mary," which left him winded until the next October. That once-a-year song was about the extent of his campaigning, but it had always been enough to win reelection against nobody.

But in the days that followed the attack, one of the first things we had to reconsider was what would happen if something bad were to happen right here. *Really* bad. *Final Days* bad. Would our mayor be capable of leading us into global, perhaps even cosmic conflict? He couldn't've fought an Arab if his life depended on it. It was a miracle he'd fought off Joe Camel this long. The world had changed, so didn't that mean we needed to change, too? To act decisively, or even overreact? It seemed likely. But Buck, though a coot, was still our coot and had feelings, so even as our anxieties about the fate of Christian democracy and the inevitability of Arab attack began to rise, we kept them hidden, which made them rise, which we kept hidden, which made them rise, which we kept hidden. That's how things build up, get reckless, in a town like ours.

Then in the first week in October, 2001, our reckless quiet found the volume knob when Wayne H. Butts entered the mayoral race.

All of us knew Wayne Butts, or thought we did, and none of us cared for him much, or we didn't think we did. He ran a shop in town, vacuum cleaner sales and repair, dealing in barely-rebuilt old console models that couldn't suck dirt out of a sandbox. He went to church Sunday mornings but wasn't what you'd call a missionary. His wife was active in the community as a gossip. The two of them dressed in old polyester patterns that had been dizzying even when they were new, and they rode around town in a beat-up Ford Falcon. He'd bought his wife a facelift for her fiftieth birthday that made her look on the verge of constant orgasm.

First light of the first Monday in October, Wayne and his wife steered their old Falcon down to the courthouse and filled out the necessary paperwork for a mayoral run—after the staff finally found some of the forms, yellowing in the bottom of a closet. Then they drove down to our local unpowerful FM station, where Wayne announced himself a candidate for mayor during the ten to eleven-thirty installment of Tradeo.

"We all *know* who's behind this," Wayne said. "I mean, *don't* we?"

"It's the Moslems," Shirley Butts said.

"That's right, it's the *Moslems*." Wayne sounded indignant and incensed—you could almost see him sitting there in the studios, sputtering on, running a white handkerchief over his fat ham face for effect, the sensory power of FM radio. "This world has changed, and we all watched it happen. Now old-fashioned values don't look so old-fashioned anymore. Now our security can no longer be taken for granted. And our very way of life, our *Christian* way of life, wherein people have the right to worship in whatever Protestant way they choose, or no way at all, at your own risk, suddenly this inalien right has been attacked. But it's not just the Moslems. It's our hedonism, our paganism, our humanism, our lack of uncompromising fundamentalism. *They've* got the fundamentalism. What do we have? Shirley, hon? Do you have something you want to say?"

Shirley leaned in close to her microphone, making it squeal. "I think it's time for dynamic new leadership," she said.

Tradeo went to the phone lines, white-hot with calls: push mower, gas powered, needed some work, fifteen dollars or would trade for push mower, gas powered, worked all the time. Then a few calls from people who were surprised Wayne Butts was running for mayor against Buck, but these people said they liked what Wayne had to say, that it was refreshing to hear a candidate who based his beliefs on what he believed rather than straight facts. A few more fearful and passionate callers added to Wayne's basic argument, saying that we had the attack coming to us, God had sent it, for the gays and the abortion and thong underwear, and they urged him to keep on telling the truth. Then four hand towels, incredibly used, Elmer Fudd print. Would trade for absolutely anything.

"Let me say, I've known our *former* mayor for many years," Wayne Butts said. "And he's been a great mayor, in those times when we didn't really need a mayor. But now we've got *Moslems* coming. They're a religious army that's going to attack us because God loves the United States. And we were *founded* on the principles of God. Now, I'm not proposing anything too drastic for our great town here. All I'm saying is that we shift our form of government to the far right, reform our public education, remove contraception from the Revco, so the kids can't have sex, and declare ourselves the first town in the country openly devoted to the teachings of Jesus Christ, as interpreted by us and people like us. Now if that's crazy, call me a dangerous nutjob. Who's with me?"

By ELECTION DAY, the answer to that question was clear: We were *all* with him, every single one of us. Wayne took 3,725 votes to Buck's zero, with one sole abstention, probably Buck taking the high road or else completely confused.

It would have been hard *not* to vote for Wayne. His platform was one-pronged, but the prong was a good one: if we had any hopes of

winning this new kind of war, a Holy War between the infidel and us,
if we hoped to smite the Moslems and bomb them where they slept,
kill them where they ate, if we wanted to bring Jesus Christ to the
Middle East and banish the souls of all those who'd heard and still
did not believe to an everlasting suffering of blinding, blackened, fiery
torment, the only way we were going to get 'er done was to become
better Christians. It wasn't enough to have God on *our* side, Wayne
warned us—which we knew we did—we had to be on *God's* side.

Who in their right mind casts a ballot against God?

But in our defense let it be said that Wayne Butts had more
going for him than just Divine Right. He also ran an Honest-To-
God campaign. He'd printed up buttons and bought a bullhorn. He
bracketed one of those loudspeakers shaped like an anus to the roof of
his Falcon and drove down Main Street booming the sound of his voice
and his message, as well as the sounds of his driving and fumbling with
the radio, the crinkle-paper of his Hardee's breakfast biscuit wrapper,
and the occasional five-star cushion rip.

He made the Sunday-morning rounds at the churches, sported
his best awful suits, spoke from the pulpits, sat in with the choirs and
sang off-key. (Buck sat in church and held the hymnal upside down.)
Wayne went to all the restaurants in town, the Sunday buffets and the
mid-afternoon workday lunches, he interrupted dinners and shook
hands. (Buck sat in the same spot he always did and drank his coffee
with the same old men and didn't shake a single hand until Wayne
came in one afternoon and worked his way around the room, finally
reaching out for Buck's hand and asking for his vote.)

Wayne went up to and invigorated children: "Well hello there, little boys and girls," he would say. "When you die, do you want to be with *Jesus*? Or burning in a lake of fire?"

"Jeeeee-sus!" the kids would yell. The simple faith of children.

"Do you love America or Mohammed?"

"A-meeeeeeeeee-ri-ca," they said.

"Do you want to support all our brave men and women in uniform? Or do you want to give aid and comfort to the enemy?"

"Su-poooooooooooooort our brave meeeeeeeeeeeeen and wehhhhhhhhhhhhhh-men in uni-form!"

"And who do you want for mayor come, November 6?"

Dead silence.

Kids.

But the real political play of the season came on the last Saturday in October, at our all-dry Octoberfest. The fairgrounds had been bringing in the crowds all weekend, shoulder-to-shoulder with men and women who wanted to forget the troubles of the world for a while, forget that our special forces had gone into Afghanistan a couple of weeks before and were finding God-Knew-What over there, men and women who wanted simply to breathe in that best fall air rich with chimney smoke, eat some fried meats, and not drink. But on Saturday night the crowd was packed more than anyone could have imagined. Some were just people who wanted to have a good time, sure, but more were there waiting to see what would happen when Buck got up to do his once-a-year half-a-verse butchering of his song. Maybe these people were undecided in their vote and wanted to see what Buck the candidate might accomplish as Buck the Entertainer, without all the mess that comes with an examination of the issues. Maybe it had nothing to do with politics but with the enjoyment of watching someone make a fool of himself in a public forum. Maybe these are the exact same thing. Regardless, the two-liter cokes flowed, the funnel cake hardened, the down-home bands took and then gave up the stage, until about 10pm when the crowd started to get excited as the headliner, the Chatahoochee Boys From Dixie, neared the end of their set and had but one more announcement to make.

"Those of y'all who are regulars know how we like to end Octoberfest," the goofy lead singer told the crowd. "Buck, where are you, son? Let's *do this.*"

The Chatahoochee Boys fired immediately into song, got the big wheel started and then kept on turnin'. Buck meandered onstage and reached a mic, started singing in the middle of a verse, bent his knees and bounced on them in a bad dance, kept time with his right hand in a judochop full of arthritis, stopped singing when he felt like it and then shuffled off stage. The Chatahoochee Boys thanked everyone for coming out tonight, and when the song finally stopped— in that big last crescendo bands do, strumming real fast and the drummer drumming nuts—an eerie silence fell upon the alcohol-free Octoberfest. Folks covered their mouths with their hands. Others cried and hugged each other tight. Still others looked up to the sky and shook their heads why, why, why? It was an inspiring display of incompetence and ineptitude, but our days of being incompetent and inept were surely over.

But then suddenly, dramatically, the breakers were breaked, the stage went completely dark, and a brief pause later a single light shone down on a ham-shaped silhouette. It was Wayne Butts, of course, strapped into a guitar.

"I hope y'all don't mind," he said. "But I'd like to sing y'all a little song, if you'd be so kind."

Before he received an answer to the question he wasn't asking, he started strumming—just him alone up there, his awful chording ability, his half-flat pitch, but delivered with great feeling—and he began to play this meaningful medley of patriotic songs, or were they gospel songs? He kept switching between the two every few words so you couldn't tell which from which, but there were eagles flying and Christian Soldiers marching, people getting washed in the blood the color of which doesn't run, and the whole thing worked its way back around to that Toby Keith song about fitting a boot up your butt.

It probably goes without saying: from there the election was a lock.

His inspired if unproficient performance, his simple act of fumbling through key changes, earned the unassuming hearts and minds of all of us present that night, even those of us who weren't there but heard about it, and he'd managed all of this in a classy, down-home manner that around here passes for masterful political theatre. Wayne soon thereafter earned the support of our local organizations, from the Legion of Decency to the Unreformed and Unpenitent Elks to the Daughters of both the American Revolution and the Confederacy. He earned the support of our local paper, the *Razorback Rag*, which gave him a rating of four fat pigs. And of course he re-reenergized the base, meaning our ministers, who rose before their congregations the morning after and told everyone that they had a moral obligation to vote in this election, and that as preachers they couldn't legally get up here and tell you who to vote for, what with the First Amendment, but if you loved the Lord and loved the United States, didn't want your children learning Arabic, and didn't like the idea of Talibon in cheap foreign-made pickup trucks cluttering up Main Street Walhalla, you should probably vote for Brother Wayne.

WHICH IS WHAT WE DID, November 6th. We went out in force, voted theocratic, and lived happily ever after. For about a month.

I guess we should've thought the whole thing through, but what did we know about theocracy? I suppose we thought it would bring a measure of perfection to our town, allowing things to become so clear that we'd no longer have to think about them. We thought it'd be like paradise, that folks would sup on milk and honey, begin dressing Amish, would bow at the waist when they met you on the street, holding their hands over their hearts in a sign of reverence and goodwill like on the Landru episode of *Star Trek*.

But in the beginning, the real shock of becoming a theocracy was that it was no real shock at all. No one dined on milk and honey, no one dressed Amish, the people who smiled at you on the street kept doing so and the a-holes stayed a-holes. In other words, our theocratic town looked a lot like our old town. I think we were a little disappointed by that, and perhaps a bit lulled by it, too. At the very least we'd expected someone from the comedy channel to send a fake reporter down here to file a story on us that made us look like idiots. But no one seemed to notice what had happened to us, not even the towns down the road. Not that they ever paid attention to us before, either.

Brother Wayne himself was to blame for some of the relative ease with which we'd made the transition. In his Election Night victory speech he'd promised sweeping reforms that would be signed into law the very next day, which was not really his first day in office, technically, but which he declared would be, a sweeping reform right there. And his first day in office he made good on this by issuing no fewer than a half-dozen proclamations, legally binding, intended to form a public policy that promised to be weirdo with his love for the Lord. He printed these proclamations out and had them tacked to telephone poles, slid under windshield wipers. He guest-hosted a half-hour show on our unpowerful FM and discussed the proclamations' ecumenical implications, as these treatises tended to be more philosophical, tackling some of the issues which displease the Lord the most, such as sex. In fact his first proclamation was released at eight in the morning sharp—he must've had it ready—and dealt with abortion and the gays. He outlawed them both outright and made strict punishments for both, which boiled down to beating the offender over the head with something, somewhere in public. But this legislation turned out to have no practical value whatsoever, as no one in town practiced either abortion or gayness. Likewise his proclamations on liberalism and moral relativism, disseminating the theory of evolution, having intimate relations with the lights turned on. None of us did any of that. Even his more practical proclamations had little practical value. He said we should construct a Town Square Christmas display that would be religious in theme and would take into account no other faith. He said we should love our neighbor as ourselves, but to report to police anyone who spoke in a foreign accent. He discouraged the intermingling of the races.

Maybe we'd been living in a theocracy all along and just didn't know it.

Meanwhile the mundane and necessary business of city government moved forward unhindered: our utilities continued to be utilized, our roads continued to be tarred, our trash pickup was unreliable as ever. Undoubtedly this was due to the fact that Wayne kept Buck's City Hall staff and asked them to keep doing whatever they did, proving their abilities to maintain civil order regardless of who filled the mayor's office, case in point Buck, who after the election went back to his lunch counter and resumed sitting, possibly not aware that he'd lost.

For these reasons above all, our transition into Jesus Town seemed an unqualified success. And as November found its full chill, our spirits found surprising warmth in a springtime of uplifting good news, which we interpreted as a sign of God being pleased with us, including our US forces moving through Afghanistan one Alhambra-sounding city at a time and Carolina beating Clemson, Hallelujah.

Our respectful nativity went up in Town Square, and the Plastic Baby Jesus never seemed so holy nor American. And of course no one was as enthused and easily re-enthused by our success than our ministers, those Grass Roots, who read each one of Brother Wayne's new proclamations from the pulpit as if it had come straight from the Press Upstairs, pointing out for their congregations the scriptural basis for each new policy or tenet or, if they couldn't find a scriptural basis, making one up on the spot.

BUT THE TRUTH about theocracy is that, once it moves beyond the abstract into the practical, it can really get a bit intrusive. Brother Wayne had spent his first month in office crusading against deviates and degenerates, doubters and disbelievers, creeps of all sort, which was fine with all of us, since nobody much fit those categories. But then Brother Wayne changed his tack somewhat and turned his attention toward us.

He began by going on Tradeo and denouncing our patriotism.

"We are in a *war*," he reminded the listening audience helpfully. "But do you know how many yellow ribbons I saw on the asses of cars on the way over here? Do you know? Twenty or so, twenty-five, maybe thirty tops. Maybe thirty-seven or forty. And do you know how many American flags I saw flying from homes or mobile homes? About as many. What's *wrong* with you people? Am I to assume that those of you who don't have a yellow ribbon bumper sticker don't support the war, don't support our troops, and are in fact dangerous dissenters? Yes, I think that's fair. I want to see some *patriotism* here, people. I want to see some unity that borders on reckless. From this moment on, I decree that you *must* put a bumper sticker on your car, which you can purchase at City Hall for $10.99. I assure you, proceeds from the sale—and it's just about all profit on these things—will go toward some legitimate thing for our town. I'll figure out what once I see the cash."

Brother Wayne had even put some thought into the design: they were yellow ribbon stickers. They were stickers shaped like yellow ribbons. You know. Though he'd put a cross in the middle to make his point.

Of course, those of us who hadn't stickered our bumpers hadn't not done it because we didn't support the troops or the war, but because we didn't like shit on our bumpers. It had merely been a matter of personal choice. Still, it was a decent-looking sticker, and you could be fined for not having it, so we were happy to slap it on. The demand for these stickers grew so great—by law—that Brother Wayne designed an entire line of patriotic paraphernalia, from flag pins to keychains to leisurewear. He put out a Xeroxed catalog at taxpayer expense. He himself modeled the men's suit. It was the style of suit he always wore, except for dizzying plaid it was thirteen stripes, fifty blue stars, and a tie with one crazed-looking eagle. Sister Shirley modeled the women's wear, what looked to be three big flags stitched together in a boxy loose-fitting gown that stretched from shoulders to floor, with enough material left over to wrap around the head, covering everything but a slit for her eyes.

Still, his poor-selling items were not his dumbest idea.

His dumbest might've been to pick a fight with our high school mascot.

He'd stormed into Tradeo one morning claiming to have stayed up all night reading his Bible and praying for guidance when Leviticus struck him and made him suddenly realize the problem with our football program, the state's losingest. "Do you know what God writes in the Bible about *pigs*?" he spat onto the microphone. "He calls them *swine*. He says they have a split hoof but do not chew the cud. I don't think it takes a scholar to see what I'm saying here. Our mascot is the *Razorback*." His voice was full of tin and fumbling, nervous as car keys. "It's not bad enough a football is a pigskin, but to call our team the *Razorbacks*? Do you people wonder why our team is so completely assed-out? It's the same reason winning athletes being interviewed after a big game thank Jesus Christ for the victory. Because Jesus Christ *has been watching* and has used his supernatural powers to *affect the outcome of the game*. That's why we produce the worst high school athletes in the state! It's the *Razorback*. It's not because our players are *smokers*."

Tradeo went to the phone lines and people were a tad unreceptive.

"What are you *talking* about?" the callers all said. "We've been the Razorbacks forever. *I'm* a Razorback."

"Then you're an abomination to God," Brother Wayne said.

"My daddy was a Razorback." Or,

"I don't see anything wrong with it. It's for the *kids*." And,

"You're not a Back Booster. You're a Back *Buster*."

"How are these people getting through, Hicks?" Brother Wayne demanded of the host. "Don't you have some sort of screening process?"

"This is Tradeo," the old host said.

The mayor shuffled up his King James and his briefcase of notes and left in a huff.

For the rest of the show the citizens of Walhalla called in to bash Brother Wayne over the head with his own thick dumbness via that forum of democratic debate and good-natured character assassination that is FM talk radio. Most people called up chuckling. A few called pissed. But the fact of the matter was there'd been no harm done. It had been a useful exercise, really, to find out where the lines were drawn.

The next morning, we woke to the Seraphim. The Walhalla Seraphim. Every public Razorback in town had been replaced by a hideous dark scaled serpentine angel with six wings and four heads and a demonic grin. When the football coach got to school and saw the thing sticking off the front sign he stumped up and tried to pry it off with his can o bean fingers, but it appeared to be protected by an electric shock of some kind he couldn't figure out.

Then there was the time, not long after, when Brother Wayne outlawed almost everything.

This was on the early morning of Monday, December 17th, when Brother Wayne dashed off a quick handwritten proclamation For Immediate Release—he'd learned his lesson about using public forums, and would stick to undemocratic prose from this point on—in which he ordered the Walhalla Police Department, the entire force, both of them, to raid the local convenience store of its Busch Light, gentlemen's magazines, and flashing boob lighters in the first salvo in the War on Hedonism. The cops were further ordered to raid the local video store of everything you'd be embarrassed to watch in front of your mother, which turned out to be, in City Hall's judgment, just about everything on the shelves. The police left only the family-friendly entertainment: the documentaries on sharks and the Civil War, the *Best of the Best of Andy Griffith*, and the harmless animated children's programs on Noah's Ark, Jonah and the Whale, the Passion of the Christ.

Immediately the talk began around town, the telling and retelling of what happened, the constructed and reconstructed accounts of the handwritten proclamation that preceded the conflict, even seemingly firsthand accounts of the raids themselves, though from people who had been nowhere present, because we really like our hearsay.

In the first case, Herschel Mathers, the owner of the Super Convenience Mart, had been irate and tried to block the police, arguing with them the entire time he was plundered of his merchandise. He said he had a *right* to sell these items, he had a license to sell alcohol by authority of both the state of South Carolina and the Federal government, and he pointed to it, framed on the wall. He said ATF controls all that, and SLED. He kept saying, this is a Federal case, this is a Federal case, and he kept saying that same thing even as the cops pulled away with two black-and-whites' worth of his hedonistic stuff. Across town, Big Homely Ed of Big Homely Ed's Video had taken it even worse, calling up people despondently, trying to tell them he'd been robbed, he'd been robbed, but he couldn't really further the story in any meaningful way because he was sobbing too hard.

Is this the point where things went too far? Is this the point where our town stood up to the strong-arm tactics of City Hall and reclaimed ourselves as a democracy? No, because we were afraid to do so, for fear of sounding unpatriotic, or maybe I mean unchristian. And the reason governments like that exist is because people keep quiet, and the reason people keep quiet is because governments like that exist. (We've since put that on a bumper sticker ourselves, $10.99, looks sharp.) Even our paper, the *Razorback Rag*, refused to stand up to City Hall's overreaching. In fact they'd quickly changed their name in all the pig discussion to simply *RR*, like a humor magazine, or a pirate one, though they insisted they'd not changed their name at all but merely their logo, for the same reason no one wants to eat Kentucky Fried Rat.

Regardless, the town of West Union is three miles down the road, where you could buy beer and booby lighters and rent steamy videos all at the Jumbo King, and eat a hamburger, too, if you wanted. The only people directly put out were Herschel and Big Homely Ed, both of whom we felt sorry for, sure, but their government-imposed cleanouts had been like a form of Eminent Domain, many rationalized.

In church the following Sunday, Christmas Eve Eve, our ministers put their best faces on Brother Wayne's reforms. They claimed that a War on Hedonism, the hot new catch-phrase, was a good thing, a sign of ethical progress for our town. And even if the measures used to fight the war might seem a bit extreme—raiding sovereign businesses, for one—the results were likely pleasing to the Lord.

"They took all our beer," some in the congregation said.

"I think that's wonderful," the ministers said. "Banish the demon drink far away!"

"They took all the movies."

"The filmcapades of Hollywood and Gomorrah," the ministers said.

"They said they know who amongst us rented those *Women's Prison* movies."

"Um," the ministers said. "Well."

But the point is, we let it all happen. We accepted each new intrusion and thus invited the next. So when something truly hideous and in need of attention came walking up the street—when the line got crossed for good—most of us were too afraid to do anything but look the other way.

ON CHRISTMAS EVE, Brother Wayne issued a new proclamation to help further define his previous one. It was posted on the World Wide Web, stapled to telephone poles; it blew with the wind down Main Street like tumbleweed. It read, in its entirety:

To: The Town of Walhalla

From: Wayne H. Butts, Mayor

Re: War On Hedon

Merry Christmas!

Last week I issued a statement regarding Hedonism, declaring open war on it in our town. So far I have seen signs of good progress. Or I thought that I had, by removing those things that corrupt the soul, such as alcohol and cinema. But then I got to thinking, I wasn't really hitting the problem. Declaring a War on Hedonism is a good idea, but when it comes right down to it, it was a dumb idea, because I'm missing the target. I'm fighting symptoms of a disease rather than the cause. Removing Busch Light doesn't do anything for that. The cause of sin is the Devil and I fight the Devil every day. I'm fighting him even as I type this out, *hard*. But I can't kill the Devil, so I have to look for Plan B, and the next obvious cause of disease is that crud in every one of your black hearts. Your secret sins. Your fun sins, your pet sins, all that human nature. How does one fight secret sin? If secret sin is the cause of external, seeable sin? I have a plan. Operation Righteous Indignation is over, and now Operation Exposure to the Light of Day is begun. What this means is, when you offend God in some way, you will be issued a ticket. But then I thought that a ticket isn't good enough. You can throw that away. What really conquers sin and vanishes evil? What gets to the root of it and snaps it? The only one thing I know of, which is the blood of the Lamb. Also, public shame. That's where I'm going with this.

From now on, when you get caught doing something, you will be issued a sign to wear. Open container, you'll be given a sign to hang around your neck telling people you're a damn drunk. Parking violation, that's a sign, maybe Doesn't Follow Directions. But whatever you get caught with, or doing, we'll determine the sin and post it on you. I mean, let's be real, DUIs get a yellow tag and pervs get a yard sign, and that's *already*, in the whole country. It's a very American thing I'm talking about here, and it goes back to the righteousness of our forebears and pilgrims. It's a vision of America. I'm not calling you drunk-driving pervs, but your sin is going to hang around your neck, whatever it is.

But then, I thought, or I'm thinking right now, that signs can be thrown away just as easy as a ticket, so how about something you're stuck with and can't lose or hide?

How about a big wooden cross? Not so big you can't carry it, but big enough to be a complete annoyance. Cumbersome. I'll get right on that. And when you get a ticket in the next few days for your secret sins, take these tickets into City Hall and redeem them for your cross. And your cross, in turn, will redeem YOU. Those of you who think I'm kidding can go jump. If you think I'm crazy go jump again. You elected me, and if I'm so crazy what does that say about you, smart guy?

I see nothing blasphemous about this idea.

In Love of the Lord,

Wayne

Appended to the bottom of the letter was a picture of Wayne and Shirley, their Christmas card. This was the first real close look many of us had gotten of Wayne since the election. His hairline had sunken back in his forehead and his eyes looked full-on black, as if removed, rolled in oil, and repotted back into his head. Shirley stood beside him but at a distance, hoping to sneak sideways out of the frame. Her frown was difficult to interpret, of course, because of the facelift.

Our Christmas Days were contained, paranoid affairs, wondering with each new gift unwrapped what secret sin had just been revealed. Whether our wife's selfless gift-giving exposed our pride in the form of a monogrammed bowling ball, as well as revealing perhaps our sloth and drunkenness. Whether our gifts of silk pajamas to them revealed both our lust and our tendency to give gifts to our wives that gave back to us. We worried about our children, second-guessing the fake costume jewelry, pink boa, and blood-red lipstick of the "How Old Am I Again?" playset, and we double-checked the rating on those Xboxes to find they contained extreme gore and violence, adult language, adult situations, and plenty of malicious intent.

Across town our ministers spent their Christmases in the same state of apprehension, hunkered down in their own modest homes festering holiday ulcers that had nothing to do with gravy. In fact they'd not been able to eat a single sprinkled cookie, nor enjoy the thinnest cut of ham. Something was clearly off.

Our dreams over the holiday were the worst of all, sugarplumless and strange, crucified and unseasonal, chalk-dust dreams of a barefooted Savior on a Holy Land road, dragging His own heavy death toward Golgotha. It was the worst Christmas ever.

ON THE MORNING of the 26th, the first of our citizenry began bearing a cross. It was for noise violation, gross intoxication, and the discharging of firearms. Etched across the horizontal bar was a single word: Roughneck. Billy Giles, the offender, had thrown the cross into the bed of his pickup and was driving it up and down Main Street, half-hanging out his window, thumbing back for people to take a look at it. I think he was proud.

Billy and his brothers spent every Christmas Night hanging out at their farmhouse getting pissed on OFC whiskey, and once their judgment was fully impaired they broke out the shotguns and took turns in the backyard firing off shells at nothing in particular. From what we'd heard, they'd spent the beginning of *this* Christmas Night like the rest of us, in quiet and worried contemplation over current events, except they decided to break out the OFC anyway. Then, after a few pulls off the bottle, they wondered what would really happen if they *did* get ticketed. After all, if they didn't get fall-down drunk and fire off a few rounds on Christmas, hadn't the terrorists already won? So they stopped thinking and started drinking in earnest, and just after midnight, duck-for-your-lives season was open. Where the three other Giles boys were that morning, and thus the three other crosses, we didn't know. Maybe they were still sleeping it off. Either that, in jail, or at the ER getting a finger sewed back on. But Billy didn't seem too worried about it. It was the only time he'd been first in anything.

But then by mid-morning there were a few more—simple infractions, a speeding ticket, a library fine, that kind of thing—and then, a few more. In the holiday post-bustle, it was something interesting to watch. It was even, perhaps, mildly funny. Had we been scared of *this*? Harmless public humiliation? The steps of City Hall became a runway for disbelieving perp walks, otherwise upstanding men and women with their heads hung low, muttering to themselves. It was almost like a guilty pleasure to watch, so a few people started standing outside City Hall and rubbernecking. Then someone from City Hall came out and issued them a ticket for the rubbernecking, and these people did their perp walks inside. Their crosses said, Judge Not.

By nightfall City Hall had formed a line. It moved an inch at a time and reached a block back. It shuffled straight ahead without conversation, like a line you'd see in Warsaw in black-and-white film reels, rather than Walhalla. Many of the same men and women standing there, sunken faced, had been mildly entertained by the whole business earlier in the day, when it had been someone else's sin. Behind City Hall one could hear the sound of incessant hammering, nailing, sawing, two or three or more carpenters back there, unseen, churning out crosses the way carpenters in old Westerns churn out coffins. Brother Wayne's office light, facing east toward the road, burned on into the small hours. Every now and then you could see him, a fat dark shape moving quickly past the pane.

Obviously we had a problem, but we didn't know just how big a problem until the next morning, the 27th, when sunrise revealed a town absolutely clumsy with crosses. They were leaned on buildings, abandoned on streets, planted into the lawn-space around City Hall, for temporary measures, but the image was enough to chill your blood. Town Square looked to be a loading-zone for shame. Crosses were strapped to the hoods of cars or stuck halfway out of barely-closed trunks. It looked like a Holy Land gift shop had exploded over our town. And most distressing, the line standing in front of City Hall was twice as long and twice as slow as it had been the day before, seemingly overnight.

Then as people began talking and spreading whatever rumors they had, we learned that there as nothing "seemingly" about "overnight"— Brother Wayne had indeed ordered his police force out on nighttime door-to-door, room-to-room campaigns across town, conducting raids without warrants or due process on sleepy-eyed, confused citizens and their private property, rummaging through closets and drawers for signs of some ticketable offense.

But that didn't make sense, we pressed these rumorers. Our town had two, count-em two, cops, and if you put them both together, you'd still get only about half a cop. How could they have the time or energy to go door-to-door, issuing this many tickets?

It was because—the rumorers told us—Brother Wayne had brought in some fresh blood. Brand new members of the Walhalla PD . . . dressed all in black, no badge, no insignia, not even a gun belt that anyone saw. Eyewitnesses recalled them as bone-thin and tall, maybe seven feet, stickfigure men seeming to be from some other part of the world—not that they looked Asian or Norwegian but that they had some trait that was hard to identify. They had hollow sockets and starved cheeks, as if they'd all been held upside down and drained of their blood. They spoke in a dialect like outer space music. There were either four of them total, who worked their way miraculously across town—one minute on the far side, the next on the near—or there were multiple groups of the same four. One of the four always asked the lady of the house for coffee, meaning the can full of grounds that he could eat with a spoon.

Then there'd apparently been some confusion as to the whereabouts of our own Brother Wayne that night, too. His office light stayed on until morning, a single glowing eye facing the street and overlooking the fenced-in rear of the courthouse, where stand-up lights had been brought in for the carpenters working on crosses, casting a red, rolling fog so that they could keep on making racket, even though they were likely half-dead from exertion. And it was clear that Brother Wayne had been in his office all night, people said—he'd occasionally drift past the window and cast his foul shadow—but then several others claimed to have spotted Brother Wayne in different parts of the town overnight, at more or less at the same time. Some claimed to have seen him north toward the mountain, walking along the dark road which led to our spooky State Park forest, rumored to be home to devil worshippers, confederate ghosts, certainly a Deliverance-level cracker or two. One such eyewitness was Beulah Leigh, who leaned out her window and called out to Brother Wayne prithee—she actually said, Hey there mayor whatcha doin walkin' up the mountain without reflective gear?—and whose prithee went unreturned.

Over by Dairy Queen, someone claimed to've seen Brother Wayne 'round midnight walking the train tracks, accompanied by a much larger and harder-to-see individual who looked like a cross between a linebacker and a hunchbacker and who walked hobbled up, sort of like a goat-man. Again the spotter called out to Brother Wayne, which the mayor left unrecognized and unreturned. Maybe Brother Wayne had been consorting with God-knows-what kind of corruption and sleaze; he was, after all, a used vacuum cleaner salesman. Maybe he had a twin brother, one of them good, the other of them evil and mustachioed, and our town was being torn apart in their yin-yang struggle. Maybe Brother Wayne had figured out teleportation. Maybe so.

Though to be honest, this rumormongering really didn't do that much for us; for the men and women of our town who were called upon to take up their cross, what mattered was not where Brother Wayne had spent his night, or to which agency or entity he'd sold his soul, but figuring out what could be done to derail the runaway train of brute force and moral authority that had become our government.

By the 28th some in our town had taken up that question with full force. A few began standing outside City Hall holding up signs protesting Operation Exposure to the Light of Day, publicly questioning Brother Wayne's tactics and theology, even his qualifications for being mayor, much less a mouthpiece for Jehovah. A few more among us—the most high-falutin' and humanistic—began preaching a gospel of peaceful and mindful resistance, claiming that corrupt governments are sanctioned by public apathy, by acquiescence, and that the simple act of refusing to participate could change the system. Of course City Hall tried to discredit these broadminded radicals as quickly as possible, all of them schoolteachers, librarians, people who could read, by issuing more crosses. Those who publicly criticized City Hall's tactics would be issued a cross that read, Agitator. Those who flat refused, Traitor. Failure to pick up your cross would result in its going back to the woodshed, where carved beneath your original sin it would now also read, Failure to Pick Up Cross.

But our broadminded radicals would not be denied. They formed a picket line five or six strong, they trained each other in how to bear a serious blow to the head. They broke out their posterboard and sharpies and their wooden sticks and their acoustic guitars, and for good measure they brought out thick logging chains, in case they needed to chain themselves to something. They sang We Shall Overcome, though they only knew those three words and hummed the rest, and even those three of the Negro spiritual chorus and title could really only be mouthed for justice, versus the sound of constant carpentry behind City Hall.

Yet here's the surprising thing: It almost worked.

Even these small acts of civil disobedience began to have what they call a rippling effect. Every time someone new refused to participate in the system, the system slowed down that much more to accommodate the refusal. Every time someone from City Hall would walk across the street and tell our radicals, "Your cross is ready," and every time our radicals would say back, "Shove it up your ass, pig," their crosses were dragged back behind City Hall for more work. Thus it was gridlock. It was cross-lock. It was subtle and patriotic sabotage. Believe me, no one was more surprised by this than our broadminded radicals, whose resistance had been intended more or less as a meaningless, bloodless gesture, which is how broadminded radicals like to fight. But this time, we couldn't believe it, their passive Ghandi hand-wringing had shown some real-world results, like the germs accidentally killing the aliens in *War of the Worlds*.

Brother Wayne tried his best to remain on-message even as the hammering and nailing slowed and stopped. He tried his best to ignore reality and stick stubbornly to his plan. He grabbed his old campaign bullhorn and leaned out his office window and bellowed for our hippies to come get their damn crosses. But by this time it was no use. By that point we'd tasted freedom, democracy had taken root, and besides, City Hall was running out of carpenters, as one had to be airlifted to Oconee Memorial that Saturday the 29th with chest pains. The line in front of City Hall broke rank, ripped up their violations, and returned home. Our sanitation department looked at the mess of crosses on Main Street and groaned.

BUT BROTHER WAYNE had always been—at least since he'd been elected—a man with his blinders on. His right eye didn't know what his left eye was doing. His view of reality extended about two feet in front of his face. He should have taken Shirley and skipped town, sneaked into exile further south, maybe somewhere near Columbia, where nobody would ever care to look. Instead that night Brother Wayne sent out his four policemen—who despite being thin and French-like were strong as ox—to drag everyone who'd refused to pick up their cross into Town Square.

To be nailed to their cross.

Sunrise of December 30th broke in clouds of cotton-soaked blood. To the sounds of screaming, of spikes driven deep into bone. Our eighty-six-year-old dissenting librarian Mary Hatch, who had no one to come get her after being abducted in the middle of the night and crucified, had tried to walk home herself. She'd made it just a fumbling osteoporosis mile before collapsing, trailing blood across the sidewalks and pavement. We tried to wrestle her into the back of one of our pickups, to get a shawl over her bare shoulders—the shawl, of course, would not reach around the cross—tried to get her safely back home so we could use some pliers to free her before she bled out. And as we stood there trying to help, Brother Wayne's City Hall flunkies came around tacking fliers to telephone poles, one final proclamation marked For Immediate Release. In it, he said the War on Human Nature was going well. That exposing secret sin had made us stronger. He said that heretofore City Hall would get rid of all unclaimed crosses by nailing them straight to their rightful owners. And he said that, effective immediately, in order to Keep Walhalla Green, he'd discontinued the manufacture of brand new crosses. From now on when you received a ticket, you could bring it on down to City Hall to have your sin tattooed on you: One on the forehead, one on the forearm, and one on the palm of your hand.

Our ministers read this proclamation aloud at church later that morning—packed wall-to-wall with the same kinds of crowds we'd seen right after 9/11—and finally admitted their mistake.

"We thought a theocratic town would be a good idea," our ministers said. "And more important, we thought Brother Wayne was the kind of man who could make it work. But now we have come to a different conclusion altogether about Brother Wayne. We have come to believe that he is really the Anti-Christ.

"He'll *never* give up his power, brothers and sisters. He'll say that we got what we deserved for voting for him. But tattooing on the forehead is a sure-fire sign of demonism. He's in league with the Devil. Which means, of course, there's only one thing we can do, brethren:

"Go get your weapons! Brandish your firearms! Go get the armaments you purchased to fight the Arabs! And bring them here, to our churches! We will fortify and march on Main Street! We will rescue this town from the goat-claw clutches of Satan! This is a Holy War! Between Good and Evil! And our very *souls* are at stake."

It was a relief to hear a public official make so much sense.

So we drove home from church, took off our Sunday best, and dug out our fatigues.

We armed ourselves with handguns, semi and fully-automatic rifles, shotguns, grenades, throwing stars, then piled into our respective church vans and charged toward Main Street at speeds that reached upwards of thirty-five miles an hour. The rattle of automatic rifles chattered all that day and into the night. Our young men in town took up arms with us, some as young as twelve, though all of them had fired automatic weapons before. We told them that what they did was for God, for our town, but not to get hurt or their mothers would kill us. We let them smoke cigarettes and tie dirty bandannas around their heads.

In this manner we reclaimed Walhalla block by block, fighting off Brother Wayne's groups of four out-of-town policemen all the way. It really wasn't so hard to get past them. Once you killed one of the four, the other three ran around in circles, bumping into each other like defective toys. Then you could just move past them if you wanted, on to the next block of four policemen, or you could pause for a moment and slay the other three, just for emphasis. Which is what a lot of us decided to do.

Just before midnight we reached our beleaguered City Hall, which in the not-even-two months since the election looked broken and sunken in, the boards sagging like being pulled by the balls down toward Hell, and the hordes of us surrounded the buzzard-cawing building and readied for an apocalyptic battle against ultimate evil. We were scared, sure, because as regards how to fight ultimate evil, we had no idea—some were convinced Brother Wayne would simply clop out of City Hall on his woolly Pan legs and vaporize us with a thought—though we all believed in the power of the Second Amendment, and we hoped violence would do the trick. A few had brought along pitchforks and waved them in the air like a late-night creature feature. Many more, it seemed, had brought along their Bibles and held them in the air like John Cusack holds up the radio in that movie, as if trying to perform a long-distance, radio-wave exorcism, or else they held the books in front of themselves like a shield that would withstand anything; even some of our most agnostic and liberal had a copy of the King James under their arms just in case, what they call Pascal's Wager.

But, as it turns out, we didn't have to fire a single shot at City Hall to win back our town. We didn't hurl our pitchforks or drive a stake through anyone's heart, didn't cut off anyone's head. Instead when the doors to City Hall screeched open, the Town Square clock striking iron midnight, what emerged from the doors was just a pasty little lawyer, Brother Wayne's legal counsel, who held up a copy of the town Constitution, a document that had grown in the last two months into a tome the size of *Moby Dick*, and reminded us that everything Brother Wayne Butts had done for us, and to us, we'd all agreed to.

"Pursuant to article this and that," the lawyer read, "by the power invested him by the town of Walhalla and its citizens, in all that legislation you monkeys signed off on, remember?"—he cited chapter and verse until we were all thoroughly confused, and then he took off his round-wire glasses and cleaned them on his tie—"Mayor Butts has officially resigned. So good luck, suckers," the lawyer said. "You ingrates are on your own."

And that was that.

YOU MIGHT THINK it would be difficult to go back to our old lives and normal routines after this ordeal . . . after all the bloodshed and lay-waste, the intolerance, injustice, and crucifixion. But that wasn't the case. In fact we pretty much just picked right up where we left off. In a couple of weeks it was like the whole thing never happened.

Some people insisted on bringing the whole thing back up, kept talking about pressing charges against Brother Wayne and bringing him to justice, even though we'd given him the legal right to do what he did. But by this time, we were all so sick of thinking about what had happened that we just wanted the matter dropped. Let's keep looking forward, we told those troublemakers who wouldn't let it die, making the troublemakers so mad the veins in their foreheads bulged like cocktail weiners. Besides, even Brother Wayne had moved on, spending some time on the lecture circuit, so we heard, charging a few thousand dollars a pop to tell his side of the story to college auditoriums full of white male students and white female students. Apparently his lectures have been received well.

Let him have his moment in the sun, we say. Why dwell on the past anyway? We finally had our lives back. People returned to drinking beer on their front porches, in their living rooms, in front of their TVs and with their children, and the beer had never seemed as cheap nor as cold. Stores began selling boob lighters again, and their fleshy shapes were never more stylized or degrading. We even found our old coot Buck sitting—well, you know where he was sitting—and we gave him his old job back. He didn't complain or hold any grudge or even act like he realized he'd ever lost the job in the first place. He's been running things for us ever since.

About the only ones among us who had any trouble readjusting were our young boys, the ones who'd been recruited to take up arms with us that day and fight. At the time they'd been remarkably pliant and enthusiastic: all we had to tell them was that they were fighting for God, that they'd be rewarded in the afterlife, and that's all it took to work them into a righteous patriotic fury, get them rattling off machine-gun fire without a thought. Once the fighting was done, though, the young boys looked confused, unsure, too easily distracted. None of them laughed at jokes anymore . . . even when you told them a knee-slapper, they just smiled this slight smile and dropped their heads and let out breaths that aped laughter but sounded more like shallow sighs.

The youngest who fought with us that day are now of football age, and on Friday nights they are the new fighting Razorbacks, still losing games by impressive margins, a Razorback tradition. At the ref's final whistle, when the score is announced apologetically on the PA, they shake off their helmets as if smothered by them, stand out on the field and stare back at us in the bleachers in a kind of dumb fog, scanning us as if searching for something, their troubled faces hard to read, their young minds somewhere else.

ACKNOWLEDGMENTS

My heartfelt thanks to everyone at Curbside Splendor who made this book possible, especially Lauryn Allison Lewis, who championed it; Victor David Giron, who made it a reality; and my amazing editor Traci Kim, who showed me the way. Special thanks to Alban Fischer for a gorgeous, striking book design, and for his endless patience in getting the book just right.

I'd like to thank the editors who first gave these stories such a good home: Gina Frangello at *The Rumpus*; Ashleigh Lambert and Dustin Luke Nelson at *InDigest*; Andrew Whitacre and Matt Borondy at *Identity Theory*; Traci Kim for the anthology *Amsterdamned If You Do*; Alice Pope at *Fresh Boiled Peanuts*; Mark Halliday at *New Ohio Review*; Wayne Chapman and Keith Lee Morris at *The South Carolina Review*; Nina Bayer at *Lunch Hour Stories*; and Russell Roland at *Stone's Throw Magazine*.

My gratitude to the many friends, fellow artists, and former professors who've offered me support over the years, and/or with this book in particular: Lauren Bailey, Wayne Chapman, mentor and friend Brock Clarke, Alex Debonis, Sarah Domet, Darrin Doyle, Eric Goodman, Michael Griffith, Mystie Hood, my old buddy Michael Hughes, Michelle Lawrence, Margaret Luongo, Nicola Mason, Ron Moran, Keith Lee Morris, Kelcey Parker, Jim Schiff, Billy Simms, George Singleton, Amber Sparks, Heather Totten, Lee Upton, Jessica Vozel, and Harold Woodell.

Thank you to my family for always having your arms outstretched, and in just the right place, to catch me whenever I'm about to hit the ground.

Thank you to the English departments at Clemson University and the University of Cincinnati for teaching me what I know, and to my generous colleagues at Miami University of Ohio for the opportunity to pass it on.

Many thanks to the fine people at Caribou Coffee on 747 in West Chester for keeping me fully caffeinated, rather than having me arrested for loitering. Though I know it's crossed your minds.

And my sincere thanks to you, holding this book. I appreciate it.

ABOUT THE AUTHOR

Joseph Bates's short fiction has appeared in such journals as *New Ohio Review*, *Identity Theory*, *The Rumpus*, *South Carolina Review*, and *InDigest Magazine*. He is the author of *The Nighttime Novelist*, published in 2010 by Writer's Digest Books, and teaches in the creative writing program at Miami University in Oxford, Ohio. Visit him online at www.josephbates.net.

WWW.CURBSIDESPLENDOR.COM